My Wife's INFERNO

9 CIRCLES OF PLEASURE

EROTICA SHORT STORIES, VOL. 19

Just Plain Bob

WARNING

This book contains sexually explicit scenes and adult language. It may be considered offensive to some readers. This book is for sale to adults ONLY.

Please store your files wisely where they cannot be accessed by underage readers.

About the Publisher

4Fun Publishing, a member of **BLVNP Incorporated**, 340 S. Lemon #6200, Walnut CA 91789, info@blvnp.com / legal@blvnp.com
NOTE: Due to the highly emotional reaction of some people to works of erotic fiction, any email sent to the above address that contains foul language or religious references is automatically deleted by our anti-spam software and will not be seen. All other communications are welcome.

DISCLAIMER

Please don't be stupid and kill yourself. This book is a work of FICTION. Do not try any new sexual practice that you find in this book. It is fiction and not to be confused with reality. Neither the author nor the publisher or its associates assume any responsibility for any loss, injury, death or legal consequences resulting from acting on the contents in this book. Every character in this book is over 18 years of age. The author's opinions are not to be construed as the opinions of the publisher. The material in this book is for entertainment purposes ONLY. Enjoy.

Erotica Short Stories, Vol. 19

My Wife's Inferno

9 Circles Of Pleasure

By: Just Plain Bob

© **Just Plain Bob 2015**
ISBN: 978-1-68030-359-9

Fiona

It was just another boring cocktail party until she walked in. I saw her look around with a "Why in the hell am I here" look on her face and then our eyes met. I'll swear to my dying day that a spark jumped between us.

She made her way toward the makeshift bar and I excused myself from the group I'd been talking with and headed for her. I moved next to her at the bar and before she had a chance to order herself a drink I said:

"You don't want to be here any more than I do. May I suggest that we leave and go someplace where we can get to know each other?"

I saw the smile behind the cool, appraising glance she gave me and then she said, "Do you have any place in particular in mind?"

"Well, it is too soon in our relationship to ask your place or mine, so I was thinking about some place close by. Maybe Mario's? They make a killer martini there and it's just around the corner."

Over martinis I learned that her name was Fiona, that she was twenty-seven years old and that she made her living as a painter of portraits, still-lifes and landscapes. When I asked her if there were any men in her life she looked me right in the eye and said, "Not until now."

"Does this mean that it's time for the your place or mine question?"

"How close are we to your place?"

"Fifteen minutes."

She reached for her purse, "Mine's only five – let's go."

Following her to her place I wondered what was happening to me. I've chased a lot of ladies in my time and I've been successful with quite a few, but it was never like this. Never had I looked at one and knew - just knew - that she was the one that was meant for me. And never, not ever, had things moved so quickly. From opening conversation to leaving Mario's it was less than forty-five minutes. I wondered if she too had felt the spark or whether she was just easy.

It did not take me long to find out that she was perfect for me. She unlocked the door of her apartment and was taking off her clothes before I was even inside. She pulled me toward the bedroom.

"Hurry, come on, hurry."

There was no foreplay - we hit the bed and went after each other like two people possessed and it was perfect. I instinctively knew what she wanted, where and how to touch, and she knew the same about me. The only way to describe it would be to say we fit - we were made for each other. After the first frenzied fuck she brought me back to life with the best head I'd ever gotten. Our second coupling, while not as frenzied as the first, was still intense and when it was over I surprised her by going down on her cum filled pussy. She told me later that no man had ever done that to her before. We went twice more before falling asleep wrapped up in each other's arms.

I woke to find her leaning on an elbow and looking down at me. When she saw that I was awake she said, "Will I see you again or was I wrong in thinking that something special happened between us last night?"

"I felt it, but I didn't know if you did."

"Oh I felt it all right."

We did not leave her bed until six that evening and only then because we needed something to eat besides each other. After eating we went to my apartment so I could get a change of clothes, but we were no sooner in the door than she asked me where the bedroom was. I pointed and she headed for it stripping as she walked. I had more sex that weekend than I'd had in the previous two months and I was pretty much exhausted when I dropped her off at her apartment on Sunday night. As she got out of the car she said:

"Are you sure you won't come up?"

"If I come up I'm liable to miss work tomorrow."

She laughed, "Yeah, you probably would."

"I get off work at five."

"I'm sorry baby, but I'm busy tomorrow night. How about Tuesday?"

I told her that I would see her then and I headed on home.

For the next three months Fiona and I saw each other every night but Monday and Thursday. When I asked why I couldn't see her on those days she told me that those were the two nights when people sat for portraits. I told her that I'd love to watch her work, but she said no.

"You would be too much of a distraction for me baby, and I couldn't afford to be throwing down my brushes to rip off a quick piece."

It was something that I could understand so I didn't press her on it.

At the end of three months I proposed. Given the way we felt about each other I expected the proposal to be a slam-dunk so I was stunned when Fiona said no.

"But why not? We are perfect for each other."

"I won't marry you because I don't want to give up my independence. What we have is working and I don't see any need to change things."

I worked on her for another two weeks, but she wouldn't budge on the matter. I finally decided to drop the matter before I ended up screwing up what we already had.

Another three months went by and one day I was having a business lunch with a client and I saw Fiona walk into the restaurant on the arm of a man I didn't know. Frank saw where I was looking and he smiled and said, "She really is a looker, isn't she? I wish I had the price."

"What do you mean?"

"She's a very high priced call girl. She gets five hundred for a four-hour afternoon visit and a thousand bucks for an all-nighter. Unfortunately that's way, way out of my league."

"You're joking, right?"

"No. I met her once through a mutual friend who was one of her clients."

I didn't believe him. How could I? He was talking about the woman I wanted to marry - the woman I wanted to spend the rest of my life with. Fiona and her escort sat on the opposite side of the restaurant from us and Fiona was sitting with her back to me and even though she couldn't see me, I never took my eyes off of her until it was time for me to leave.

I knew Frank was wrong, but even though I knew it, it was still in my mind and eventually human nature took over - I had to know for sure. I couldn't take time off from work during the day and I knew where she was every night but Monday and Thursday so I decided to play detective on those two nights. The next Monday found me camped out in a dark corner of her apartment parking lot. At seven I saw a man climb the stairs and knock on the door to her apartment and Fiona greeted him with a kiss and the two of them disappeared into the room. I was crushed. I doubted that kissing the customer was part of sitting for a portrait. I sat out there in my car watching the windows of Fiona's apartment for over four hours and when the lights went off and the man still hadn't come out I knew that Frank knew what he was talking about.

The next night Fiona could tell that something was wrong and she kept after me to tell her what it was. Finally I told her about my lunch with Frank, what he had said and about my night in her parking lot. I looked at her hoping that she would get mad and tell me how wrong Frank was and that she would have a perfectly good excuse for Monday night. Instead she looked away from me and said:

"I hoped that you would never find out."

"You mean it's true?"

"Yes, at least a little bit."

"What does a little bit mean?"

"It means that there is a side of me that you don't know about. Yes I used to be a high priced call girl, but I quit three years ago. That is, I quit most of it. I kept two of my regular customers."

"What is it about those two that is so special?"

"They pay extremely well and they each have something that I need."

"I don't understand."

"Well, I suppose since our relationship is pretty much toast it won't hurt to tell you. The two customers that I kept like to be bullied and humiliated and there is a part of me that has to bully and humiliate. The irony is that I could never have a serious relationship with a man who would allow me to treat him like that, but I still have the need to do it. I get some of my most intense orgasms when I fuck a man up the ass with a strap on dildo and listen to him squeal. I get off on having them under my thumb and it is a part of me that I can't give up.

"Do they fuck you?"

"Sometimes, not often, but sometimes."

I sat there looking at her and my mind was in turmoil. I had found the perfect woman for me, the woman who fit me like a glove and now I found that my perfect woman has a flaw - a serious flaw.

"I suppose that is the real reason why you won't marry me?"

Fiona nodded and said, "I know myself well enough to know that if I married you I would try to be a faithful wife, but that eventually the need to be dominant would cause a problem between us. If I tried to dominate you and you let me I would lose all respect for you and we would be finished. My only option would have been to step outside the marriage and if I did that and you found out it also would end it for us. Not getting married gave me the best of all worlds - I had my two regular wimps and, at least until now, I had you."

I was silent for several moments and then I said, "You still have me. I can't walk away from what we have. I'll find a way to come to grips with this, but I'm not going to give you up."

"I'm sorry lover, but it just won't work. Now that you know about it, it will be all you think about when I'm not with you and eventually it would poison our relationship."

"No, I don't think it would. Actually, the thought of you dominating some poor wimp turns me on."

"Oh yeah? How turned on?"

To answer her I pointed at the bulge in my trousers.

"Honey, that's just hormones. That's here and now stuff. How are you going to handle my coming home to you after one of my dates has fucked me? No baby, it just wouldn't work."

"I'm not just going to walk away. There must be some way I can show you that I won't let what you do have any effect on my feelings for you."

"Well, it would be easy enough to find out. I'll let you watch from the closet while I do my thing. I'll let him fuck me and when he is gone you can come out of the closet and eat my cum filled pussy. If you can do that you just might be able to handle what I do."

Despite the disgust I felt at seeing a grown man allow himself to be treated the way Fiona was treating him I none the less had a very stiff cock as I watched the expression on Fiona's face as she plowed the man in his ass with a 10" strap on dildo. He was squealing like a pig and begging her not to stop. His dick jutted out beneath him and leaked pre-cum on the sheets as Fiona fucked his ass and beat on his ass with a ping pong paddle. I watched, amazed, as his cock, untouched by human hands, suddenly erupted and spit cum all over the bed. The man fell forward and laid in the mess he'd just made as Fiona un-strapped the fake cock and tossed it aside.

She laid down next to the man, "Come on worm, you're not done yet. You know what you have to do now." The man got up and Fiona said, "Lick my ass and eat my pussy. If you do a good job I just might let you put your pathetic little cock in me." The man knelt between her legs and I couldn't see what he was doing, licking her ass or her pussy, but I could see her looking at the closet and smiling. After several minutes she said:

"That's enough you pathetic little freak. You may fuck me now, but be quick about it; I need to get you out of here so I can do my nails."

The man positioned himself over her and slid his cock into her pussy. Her facial expression told me that she was enjoying it, but she still continued to heap verbal abuse on the man. Even though his cock was a good seven inches and pretty fat Fiona said:

"Come on, put it in, I don't have all day."

The man was pounding into her as hard as he could and she was saying, "Are you going to fuck me or not. If you can't do any better than this you should stop and go into the bathroom and get yourself off by hand."

I saw Fiona's eyes glaze over and her nails bite into the man's ass as she had an orgasm, but I don't think he realized it as he was too wrapped up in being humiliated. I was surprised at the control Fiona had. Even as she was having her orgasm she was saying:

"Is this the best you can do? You call this fucking? No wonder your wife has to go out and fuck other men. I'll bet my fifteen-year-old paper boy can do better and he is probably still a virgin and doesn't know what to do."

The man lasted a long time and Fiona had two more orgasms before he finally collapsed on top of her. She pushed him off of her and told him to get dressed and get out.

When he was gone I came out of the closet and Fiona was lying on the bed, legs spread and waiting for me.

"Okay baby, come on over here and clean his cum out of my pussy."

"No, I don't think so."

The smile left her face and her face turned sad, "I knew it

wouldn't work. I knew that you couldn't handle it, but then I don't suppose that any man could."

"That's not it sweetie, that's not it at all."

"I don't understand."

"It's simple sweetie. You have already admitted that you can't respect a man you can boss around so there is no way I'm going to let you tell me to come on over and eat another man's sauce out of your cunt. If you want me to eat your pussy you are going to have to ask me and ask me nice."

"The smile came back, "Please baby, will you please come over here and eat my pussy?"

"Why should I?"

"To show me that I'm yours baby, to show me that you don't mind my being a slut sometimes."

I looked at her as she lay there fingering her pussy. "All right, I'll eat your pussy, but only on one condition - you have to marry me."

She held up her arms to me, "Whatever you want baby, whatever you want."

I smiled at her, "Just you remember that," I said as I got on the bed and lowered my mouth to her sopping wet box.

End of the 1st Story

Dorthea

I stared at him, stunned to the core of my being as what he said slowly registered.

"Are you sure? I mean is there any chance a mistake has been made?

"I'm sorry, I really am. I wish it could be otherwise, but I'm absolutely sure."

My drive home was an absolute horror. How are you supposed to feel when the doctor tells you that your life is over? How do I tell my wife? How do I explain it to the kids? And why now? Did God look down on me and say, "You've had a good life George. Everything has gone your way and now it is time for me to throw some shit into the game."

One minute the perfect life and the next minute life is all but over. It wasn't fair; it just wasn't fair.

***

My life had been storybook. I was the Golden Boy. An A student from the first grade until the last day of college. I excelled at sports and I lettered in four sports in high school. I quarterbacked the football team to the school's first ever Regional title. I pitched a no-hitter and hit a home run against Jefferson – our cross town rival – the only time our school had ever beaten them. I had seventeen colleges offer me scholarships and I chose State.

The football coach took one look at me on the first day of practice and said, "You might have been a quarterback in high school son, but I see you as a receiver."

I thought that the man was crazy, but in my junior year I led the conference in catches, yards gained and touchdowns scored. I made All American in my junior and senior years and graduated from college with a 4.0 GPA. I was a first round draft pick, but I'd had enough of football and I went to work for the XYZ Corporation and in only six years I made it to Vice President of Marketing, but of all the great things that happened to me meeting Dorthea was the best.

***

We met in the sixth grade when the boy's gym teacher and the girl's gym teacher decided to combine classes and teach their students to dance. I was paired up with Dorthea and that started an off again on again relationship that culminated in our wedding two years after our college graduation. From the first time that I took Dot in my arms in that gym class I was infatuated with her. So much so that for the next year I was constantly taunted by my classmates and friends.

"Georgie likes Dorthea" and "Georgie is sweet on Dorthea" is something that I heard almost every day. Sadly, Dorthea didn't feel the same way. Oh she did like me well enough, but she liked a lot of other boys to the same extent. When her parents finally allowed her to date I was just one of many that she would go out with.

Things changed a little when I got into sports. As I became successful I also became more popular and there was a class of girls at our school (as at most schools) who liked to date and be seen with the schools athletes. As those girls began to show an interest in me so did Dorthea. I found out later (in college) from one of Dot's close girlfriends that Dot knew that I was hers and would be there when she got done playing the field. Anyway, when others started paying attention to me Dot decided that she had better take care of business before some other girl lit my fire and made me forget Dorthea.

We started going steady and were a couple almost all the way through high school. I say almost because we had all the pissy assed little arguments that teenagers have and we would break up only to get back together in a week or two. The major bone of contention was sex, or more to the point, lack of it.

Every other guy in my class, at least to hear them tell it, had been laid. If they were to be believed I was the only virgin in our class. I was constantly bombarded with things like, "Last night Becky and I went to the drive-in and she sucked my cock" or maybe, "Did you hear about Nancy? She and three guys…"

Try as I might all I could get from Dorthea was some heavy necking with some tongue every once in a while. A hand on her beast would get me slapped and she would say, "If you want a slut call Sally Murphy," and then she wouldn't talk to me for a week. About the third time that happened I did call Sally Murphy, but all that did was make things worse. For one thing, if Sally was a slut she was taking the night off on the two dates I had with her and in the second place Dorthea didn't talk to me for a month after she found out I'd been out with Sally. Then when we finally did end up talking again, we broke up for good.

"How could you do that to me?"

"It was your idea. You were the one who kept telling me to call Sally."

"But I didn't really mean it and you know it."

"All I know is that I'm fed up with being the only male senior in this class who is still a virgin."

"Well I'm sorry George, but I place a higher value on my chastity. I will not engage in recreational sex just to please someone who thinks virginity is a crime. I promised my mother that I would go to my marriage bed a virgin and I fully intend to do just that."

"Well then, I guess that puts an end to us."

"What? Why do you say that?"

"You have already told me that you are not getting married until you finish college and that is almost five years away. I'm not the least bit attached to my virginity and I'm damn sure not waiting for five more years to get rid of it."

"Then I guess we have nothing else to talk about" and she got up and walked away. Okay I thought, if that's how you want it, so be it.

***

One month later it was senior prom and I took Nancy Bickford. Dorthea went to the prom with Sammy Vine and while I tried to ignore the two of them every time I looked their way I found Dorthea looking at me. After the prom I asked Nancy which of the many parties she want to go to and she said, "The one at the motel we are going to. You did plan on fucking me tonight I hope."

I was going to argue? Nancy was tickled to death when she found out I was a virgin.

"You're my first," she said, "So we get to do it my way."

"What does that mean?"

"It means that I get to teach you how to do it the way I want."

"As opposed to?"

"Being told what to do."

I got my first blow job (the first of three that night), my first piece of ass (of four) and had my first anal sex (once). But the one thing that Nancy wanted most was to have her pussy eaten. She especially loved it when I ate her after I fucked her. I was a virgin and didn't know any better so when she told me that boys always licked up their cum after making love I believed her and did it.

It was a good thing and a bad thing. A good thing because she told all the other girls that I did it and I got real popular. A bad thing because one of the girls that heard it was Dorthea. Nancy and I dated for about a month and then she started dating a college guy and dropped me.

Nancy was no sooner out of the picture when Sarah asked me to be her date at some family thing and that night Sarah had my face between her thighs. She promptly told everyone that Nancy hadn't lied and a week after that Sammy Vine was bragging that he had copped Dorthea's cherry.

After Sarah there was Betsy, Barb and Cindy and I heard that John, Bill and Mike had nailed Dorthea. It was almost as if she was showing me that she could have one every time I had one.

One day, shortly before graduation, I was sitting in a booth at the malt shop when Dorthea slid onto the seat across from me.

"How you been?"

"Good."

"You never call me anymore."

"Got nothing to say."

"Come on George, don't be that way."

"Don't be saying that to me. You're the one who lied to me and then got up and walked away from me the last time we talked."

"I did not! I never lied to you."

"Oh no? What about "I'm going to my marriage bed a virgin and I'm not getting married until I get out of college?" What about "I will not engage in recreational sex with someone who thinks virginity is a crime?" You telling me those weren't lies? You aren't married, but you damned sure ain't a virgin anymore and you haven't even started college yet, let alone finished it. You telling me that Sammy, John, Bill and Mike can't be considered recreational sex? And I certainly noticed that you had absolutely no trouble giving Sammy what you wouldn't even consider giving me. Like I said Dot, I have no reason to call you because we have nothing to say to each other."

***

The summer between the end of high school and the start of college was a busy one for me. I was working two part time jobs trying to pay off my car and put some change in my pocket for when I got to school. I was still managing to get out two or three nights a week. Most of my dates were with girls who wanted to see for themselves if what Nancy, Sarah and a few other girls were saying was true. I didn't see Dorthea at all during that summer, but I heard that she was cutting a pretty wide swath through the boys.

Fall came, I went to college and life got a little harder. I was working a part time job, carrying a full load of sixteen credit hours and playing football. Enough girls from my old high school were attending State that I still had a sex life of sorts. What with the jobs and the course load and football practice, one night a week and one day on the weekend was about the best I could do. It wasn't much, but it was still a lot more than some other guys were getting.

Even though Dorthea was supposed to be attending State I didn't see her around and I didn't hear anything about her or what she was up to. I was curious, but I wasn't about to ask. The last thing I wanted was for someone to tell Dot, "I saw George yesterday and he was asking about you." As it turned out I needn't have worried. Family problems had kept her from starting the fall term.

She did start spring term and I saw her a time or two in passing and then one day I came out of a class and found her in the hall waiting for me.

"Can we talk?"

"About what?"

"About us."

"There hasn't been an us Dot, not since the day you said we had nothing else to talk about and then got up and walked away. And, as I remember it, what we were talking about then was the virginity that you were going to hang onto for the next five years. The same virginity that you gave up to Sammy Vine less than three months later."

"I did it to hurt you George, not because I particularly liked Sammy. It hurt me terribly when you didn't ask me to the prom and it killed me to know that you were with Nancy because I knew what the two of you would be doing before the night was over. It killed me George, because you were supposed to be mine. But I bit my lip and suffered through it because I expected you to do what you were going to do with Nancy to get rid of your cherry and then come back to me.

"Then you took up with her and then went from her to Sarah and I got mad and said "Okay, I'll show him" and I let Sammy have me. After that every time you went to a new girl I went to another guy just to show you and rub your nose in it."

"So what is this all about Dot?"

"Can we just stop throwing stones at each other Georgie? Can't we try and put us back together again?"

I really didn't know what to say to that. I missed her, I still thought about her almost all the time, she was still the best looking girl I had ever been with, but still…., shit, I didn't know.

She waited for me to answer and when I didn't she said, "What? Why can't you answer me Georgie? Is it the sex thing? Is it because Sammy got it and you didn't? Well let me tell you something sweetie, you got the better of the deal. You lost yours to one of the most experienced girls in school and from the rumors floating around you had a very good night. I, on the other hand, and Sammy too for that matter, had a lousy time. I hurt like hell and I beat on his chest so hard trying to get him to stop that he had bruises for a week. Plus I bled all over him and the seat of his father's car and he caught hell for that. And then add to that the fact that I really didn't like it."

"Then why did you keep on doing it?"

"To see if I could piss you off."

"You kept screwing Sammy, John, Bill and Mike even though you didn't like it?"

"No, it was just Sammy I didn't like it with. The others were okay."

"So you do like sex?"

"It was pretty good with Mike. It was okay with John and Bill and some others, but Sammy sucked; it was strictly wham, bam and I'll call you tomorrow."

"So just what is it that you see happening with us?"

"I have an apartment off campus and I want you to move in with me."

"How can you afford that?"

"My grandmother passed away and left me a bunch of money. That's why I didn't start until spring term; I had family business to take care of."

"You want to set up housekeeping with me?"

"Yes, and if you say yes I'm going to do my best to fuck you blind and make up for all the time we've lost."

***

She did and she had been doing her absolute best to keep on doing it for the past fourteen years. The woman spoiled me rotten. She pampered me, waited on me hand and foot, my wish was her command and all that kind of thing. Our sex life was incredible. Even after living together for four years and then being married for fourteen we still made love five and six times a week. Having four kids in the house hasn't slowed us down either. Life had been perfect, and now this.

I couldn't face Dot when I got home. One look at my face and she would have known something was wrong. To forestall things I told her that something bad had happened at work and that I had brought some work home with me and that I had to get it done before the next day. Then I went into the den, closed the door, sat down at the desk and stared at the wall.

After an hour or two of trying to make sense of what the doctor had told me and feeling sorry for myself I finally snapped out of it. I wasn't a quitter, never had been and wasn't going to start being one. I got out the Yellow Pages and began looking for doctors. I made a list of a half dozen or so and tossed it in my briefcase. I would get second, third, fourth and maybe even a dozen opinions. No way I was going to settle for just one.

The list made and my mind made up as to a course of action I left the den and went looking for Dot. If the doctor was right I might not have too many more opportunities. She was in the kitchen doing dishes and I grabbed her hand and said, "Woman, I have needs" and I dragged her along behind me to the bedroom where I let her reduce me to ruin.

Two weeks later the jury was in. Five different doctors told me the exact same thing. There was no denying it anymore. No way I could hide from it, no way to avoid it. The only thing left to do was face up to it and sit down with Dorthea and tell her. That was going to be the hardest part of the whole thing. We had been so good together. We fit like a hand in a glove; everyone said that we were the perfect couple and they all said they wished they could be like us.

***

I took a day off work so I could sit down and talk with Dot while the kids were in school. It was one conversation that I did not want interrupted. It was going to be hard enough as it was without having to stop when Alice came in the room with a, "Mommy, Josh hit me." Or maybe it would be Mary coming in, "Mommy, will you help me dress my dolly?" or Kevin wanting me to show him how to re-lace his first baseman's mitt.

I couldn't find the words. I sat there looking at the woman who had made my life sing, but I just couldn't make myself talk.

"What is it Georgie? What is this all about? Come on George, what is so important that you had to stay home just to talk to me?"

It was hard, but I finally took a deep breath, "Two weeks ago the doctor gave me some very bad news. I didn't accept it so I went to a different doctor and got a second opinion. I didn't believe him either, but after having the tests run by three more doctors I have to face up to the facts. I can't keep myself in denial and hope it will go away because it won't. It is there, it is malignant, and it is eating away at me."

"Oh my God George, what is it, cancer?"

"Of sorts Dorthea. What I have is worse than cancer. Cancer eats away at your body. What I have is infinitely worse because what I have is eating away at my soul. What I have is an unfaithful wife. When I had my yearly physical they found a spot on my prostate. They ran a whole bunch of tests on me and when they came back the doctor, who was familiar with my sports background, said that it must have been hard not to have had a son to follow in my footsteps. I asked him what he meant by that and he told me I was sterile.

"I didn't believe it Dot. How could I be sterile with four kids in the house? So I checked it out with four other doctors and they all told me the same thing. In addition I took the kids in for flu shots and had DNA tests done at the same time. According to the DNA tests Dot, the kids have four different fathers and not one of them me."

"Care to comment Dorthea?"

End of the 2nd Story

Room 123

"Honest to God Marge, I'm just hanging in there until he becomes vested in his pension plan. Then when I leave him I can get the court to award me half. What? No, I should be all right until I can land someone else. Sure. I'll get half of everything he has and the beauty of it is that the court will order him to pay my lawyer out of what he has left. No. Hey, he's a nice enough guy, but he just doesn't satisfy me sexually."

I had smashed my thumb at work and had gone to the clinic. After putting two stitches in it they had given me some pain medication and the warning label said it would probably make me drowsy and that I shouldn't drive or operate machinery. I'd come straight home from the clinic, arriving three hours before my usual time, and when I came in the front door I heard Jillian on the phone in the kitchen talking to her friend Marge. I stood silently in the living room and listened to what else my "loving wife" had to say. Of course I couldn't hear what Marge was saying, but then I didn't really have to. What I heard coming out of Jillian's mouth was pretty self-explanatory.

"No Marge, I haven't had a good fucking in two months. The last one I had was with Gerald just before he moved to St. Louis. I know, I know, but there is just something about a big cock that sets me all aquiver. Remember Tom? His was almost ten inches long.

"Remember the time we told our hubby's we were going to an Avon party? Wasn't that a wild night? I wonder if that bar is still there. It is? Hey, how would you feel about another Avon party? Really? How about Tuesday? Okay, I'll plan on it.

"Fuck no, he believes everything I tell him. The last time I fucked Gerald I had so much cum in me that I could have floated a battleship and hubby dear wanted to fuck when I got home. I told him I wanted him to eat me first and when he commented on how wet I was I told him I was all hot and wet from thinking about him all day and hoping he'd want to fuck me that night. No lie. I actually had an orgasm thinking about how wicked I was being. Okay, I'll let you go. Don't forget Tuesday, okay?"

***

I slipped back out of the house, drove a couple of blocks away and sat and waited for my regular time to go home. I thought about what I had just overheard. Apparently my ten-year-old marriage to Jillian wasn't near as good as I had thought. I wondered how long she had been hanging horns on me. From her conversation with Marge it had to be at least three years. Tom with the ten-inch cock had to be Tom Bakley, I'd seen his equipment in the locker room at the health club, and he had left town three years ago. I tried to remember the night of the so-called Avon party and while I wasn't sure I believed that it took place just a little over three years ago. Three years and I hadn't had a clue. Well, I knew now and I knew the plans that Jillian had for me. It was time for me to make some plans of my own.

Curiosity got the better of me and when Jillian told me about going to the Avon party with Marge I told her fine, that I would be working late that night and I would catch a bite to eat on the way home. Tuesday night I was in a borrowed car parked just down the street when Jillian backed out of our driveway. I followed her to Marge's place and as Marge climbed into Jillian's car I wondered if her husband was just as clueless as I had been.

I followed them across town and I began to wonder just where the hell they were going. We were moving farther and farther away from the part of town where most of the good clubs were located. They finally pulled into the parking lot at a place called Washington's Bar and Grill and I had a hard time believing that this was their destination. For one thing it was in that part of the city known as "Niggertown" and for another the place looked like a seedy dump. I pulled over, parked, and then watched as Jillian and Marge got out of the car and went inside. I settled back to wait and see what happened.

I'd been sitting there about half an hour when a cop car came slowly down the block. I saw the cop on the shotgun side take a good look at me as they went by and I was not really surprised when they came back by thirty minutes later and took another look at me. In another fifteen they were back and they pulled up behind me and parked. The two got out of the squad car and approached, one on either side, and the one on my side tapped on the window with his flashlight. I already had my driver's license out and I gave it to him before he asked for it and then he asked me what I was doing sitting in that particular neighborhood. I didn't see any reason not to tell him so I laid the whole story out for him. He asked me for a description of Jillian and then he went over and entered the bar. Five minutes later he came out carrying a white paper bag and came over to my car.

"Joint doesn't look like much, but they have the best half pound ground round in town. The two women are sitting at a table in back with six big black bucks and they were being pretty friendly, if you know what I mean. Good luck" and then he and his partner got in their car and left.

It was another hour before Jillian and Marge came out of the bar, each one arm in arm with a black dude. The four of them got in Jillian's car and drove off. I made a U-turn and followed them as far as the Castle Inn Motor Lodge. Five minutes later the four of them were in room 123 and I had seen enough. I headed on home, took a shower and went to bed. Three hours later I heard Jillian come in. She came into the bedroom and I heard her undressing and then she climbed in bed and shook my shoulder.

"Baby? Are you awake Hon?"

I rolled over, "I am now."

"I'm horny baby. I've been thinking of you all day and I'm so hot, wet and horny that I think I'll die if you don't make love to me."

She pulled my hand to her cunt and she was indeed very wet and I wondered how many times she had been cum in and whether or not it had been by both men.

"Come on baby, I need it bad."

"Not tonight Jillian. I have a headache" and I turned on my side to go back to sleep. That was the first time in our married life that I had said no to her when she wanted sex and I wondered if she was lying there looking at my back and wondering just what the hell had happened.

***

The next two weeks I was busy making arrangements and setting my plan in motion. When everything was in place I called Jillian from work and told her not to fix dinner.

"I've just been promoted sweetie and tonight we are going out to celebrate."

We had dinner at Jillian's favorite restaurant and I ordered a liter of wine to go with dinner. I barely sipped mine but I made sure that Jillian's glass was kept full. She was in a happy mood when dinner was over and then I took her out dancing and more drinking. Every drink I got Jillian was either a double or a triple and every one I got myself was plain tonic water. At ten I almost had to carry a giggling Jillian out to the car.

She didn't seem to know where she was when I pulled into the parking lot at the Castle Inn Motor Lodge and she was still giggling when I carried her from the car into room 123. I sat her down on the bed and undressed her all the while telling her how sexy she looked and how I was going to see to it that her brains were fucked out.

When she was naked I pushed her back on the bed and reached under the pillow for what I had put there earlier in the day when I had rented the room. While Jillian looked up at me and giggled I put Velcro straps around her wrists and then attached them to the eyebolts that I had installed earlier. When I pulled them tight Jillian stopped giggling and asked me what I was doing.

"Just going to help you out here sweetie."

I strapped her legs in a similar fashion and then I took one of the pillows, folded it in half and stuck it under her ass. Then I stepped back and looked at my handiwork. Jillian was spread-eagled on the bed and the pillow pushed her pussy up and made it look very accessible. Jillian was looking at me with a frightened look on her face and I smiled at her.

"So I don't satisfy you sexually? You haven't had a good fuck since Gerald moved to St. Louis, right? Those two black guys' two weeks ago didn't get the job done? Well, as a good husband it is up to me to see that my wife gets what she needs."

The frightened look was replaced with one of panic as she tugged at her restraints.

"I don't know what you are talking about, let me loose."

"Don't fight it baby, I'm just giving you what you say you want. By this time tomorrow you will be so sexually satisfied that you might not want to look at another cock for six months."

She was begging me to untie her when I put the ball gag in her mouth and the blindfold on her. I walked over to the window and pulled the blinds and I was not at all surprised to see about a dozen blacks and Mexicans standing just outside. When I rented the room I'd told the desk clerk that I was married to a rich bitch that liked to play sex games. She liked to be tied up and gangbanged by minorities and that she would do anything that anybody wanted as long as she was tied up and blindfolded.

"The first ten or so can only use her cunt, but after that the ball gag can come out and they can use her mouth. Don't pay any attention to her protests because they are just part of the game she plays. They can take any hole they want as long as the blindfold stays on and the hands stay tied."

I gave him a hundred bucks and told him to spread the word. He must have done a good job because even as I looked out the window more were arriving. I opened the door and stepped outside.

"You know the rules?" I got a lot of heads nodding yes and so I stepped aside and said, "Enjoy."

***

I sat in my car across the lot from room 123. The blinds stayed open and so did the door and I watched as cock after cock speared into Jullian. After the fifteenth one I took out my cell phone and made a call. Luckily Marge answered instead of her husband. That saved me from having to tell two lies instead of one.

"Marge? Jillian just called me and asked me to call you. She said to tell you that she was the Castle Inn Motor Lodge picking up the Avon stuff you bought the other night and she only had enough money to pick up her order and she wants you to come down and bring enough money to get your stuff."

"No, I don't know. She said she had been trying to reach you, but her cell phone is acting up."

"What?"

"Oh, she said room 123. Okay, bye."

It took forty-five minutes for Marge to show up and when she walked up to room 123 she was grabbed and pulled into the room. Within four minutes she had a cock in her cunt and her mouth. I watched for another hour as more blacks, Mexicans and Asians showed up and made deposits in room 123 and then I took out my cell phone and made another call. When Marge's husband answered I said:

"Your wife is cheating on you with a nigger. Right now she is with him in room 123 at the Castle Inn Motor Lodge on Sixth Avenue. If you hurry you can catch her in the act."

Help my wife fuck over me? Well fuck her too.

While I waited for Marge's husband to show up I went back over my moves of the previous two weeks to see if I had overlooked anything. I'd cashed out all the certificates of deposit and had taken the cash and put it in a safety deposit box that I'd rented using the name and social security number of my dead grandfather from my mother's side of the family. I had closed out the savings account and that cash had also gone into the box.

But the one that really made me smile was the deal on the house. I'd bought the house before I met Jillian and it was in my name only. I'd always meant to put Jillian's name on the title, but I just had never gotten around to doing it. I'd taken advantage of the current low interest rates and I had refinanced the house for every penny I could get out of it and that money too went into the safety deposit box. It wasn't as easy as it sounds because converting a check for two hundred thirty-five thousand into cash took some time and some doing, but I got it done.

The only thing left for me to do was cancel all the credit cards in the morning. I hadn't done it before getting her into the motel room because if she had tried to use a card she would be denied and that might make her think something was up.

When the divorce came around Jillian would indeed be entitled to half the assets according to our state law, but half of what? Half of the non-existent CDs? Half of the empty savings account? Half of what the house was worth? There wouldn't be anything left after the house was sold, the loan paid off, and the real estate commissions paid. She wouldn't even get half of my pension because I had given notice and would be leaving the job before I became vested in the pension plan. But where did it all go her lawyer would ask.

"Alas" I would say, "The gambling habit that I'd been fighting for years finally wiped me out."

In room 123 the blindfold was off, the Velcro straps untied and Jillian and Marge were being passed around like inflatable fuck dolls. There was a line of blacks, Mexicans and Asians out the door when Marge's husband pulled up. He took one look in the room and then got back in his car and drove away. I started my car and followed him out of the lot and headed home to wait for Jillian to come home and face the music. It might be a long wait - I'd rented room 123 for three days.

End of the 3rd Story

Angie's Fantasy

The things you do in your youth have a way of coming back to haunt you. Sometimes that can be a good thing, but sometimes it can fuck you up big time.

Remember when you were a teenager and desperate to get rid of your hated virginity? Remember what lengths you went to to try and get your cherry popped? Well, that was me times ten. I couldn't even get a date, let alone get laid. It didn't help that I was overweight and had pimples all over my face and that I was inordinately shy. And naïve, can't forget to mention naïve. I was so eager to please and be accepted that I was taken advantage of all the time. The one thing I had going for me was that I had a driver's license and a car. The car had been a bittersweet gift from my brother. When I was thirteen he was drafted and sent to Viet Nam and he never came back. The day I got my learner's permit my dad called me into his den and handed me a set of keys.

"Danny said that if something happened to him you were to get his car."

It took me a while before I could drive it without getting all weepy eyed, but then something happened that, I'm ashamed to admit, made me forget all about Danny. I became popular. I was suddenly everybody's good friend. It was the car of course, but that's where the naïve part came in. I thought that everyone had suddenly discovered what a great guy I was – that suddenly they had seen the 'inner me', the 'real' me. Suddenly it was, "Hey Dave, let's go to the lake this weekend," or "Dave, what do you say we catch a movie at the drive-in." I would always say yes and a bunch of kids would pile into the car and we would take off, but when we got where we were going I was still the odd man out. They weren't all one way about it; they did pay for the gas and I never had to pay my way in at the drive-in movie, but as far as getting anywhere with the opposite sex I was still batting zero. Even the times that the guys "brought along a girl for me" she always ended up with someone else. Eventually I tumbled to the fact that I was being used, but hey, any popularity was better than none.

I don't even remember how many times I drove to the drive-in and watched in the rear view as a couple made out, or watched out of the corner of my eye as a couple necked on the front seat next to me. More than once a couple actually fucked on my back seat and on those nights I would go home with a severe case of blue balls and beat my meat until it hurt.

Then came the night that changed my life.

It was a Friday night and a couple of guys asked me to take them to the drive-in. Billy Moore was in the back with Mary Koslowski and Nancy Holbrook. The front seat had Bobby Neubert and Sally Mason sitting next to me. Ten minutes into the movie I heard a low moan from the back and I looked in the mirror and saw Billy finger fucking Mary. Mary had Billy's cock in her hand and was stroking it and Nancy was watching it all with disgust all over her face. Then Nancy said, "You guys are no better than animals" and she opened the door and got out of the car. I got out to follow her. I figured that I'd catch up with her, tell her how disgusting I thought Mary and Billy's behavior was and maybe get in her good graces. I caught up with her and she turned to face me, "All of you boys are nothing but goddamned pigs. Just get away from me" and she turned and ran away.

When I got back to the car Billy was between Mary's legs and she was screaming, "Yes, yes, fuck me, fuck me." Sally was leaning over the seat watching while Bobby was fucking her from behind. When I got in the car the dome light came on and Billy hollered out, "Turn off the fucking light damn it!" I was just a little pissed at Nancy for calling me a pig when I hadn't ever done anything to her and when Billy hollered it pissed me off even more and I did something that none of them had ever seen before – I got mad!

"Fuck you! It's my car and my light and if I want to turn it on I will and if you don't like it get your ass outside and do your fucking on the ground."

I saw Bobby smile and I heard Sally giggle and Mary said, "Just shut the fuck up Billy and fuck me."

The two couples managed to get their rocks off and then they settled in to watch the movie. Within ten minutes they were necking again and within twenty they were fucking again. Sally and Bobby finished and were sitting there smooching when the movie ended and the lights came on. Mary and Billy were still going at it when all of a sudden I heard Mary cry out, "No god damn it, no. I'm almost there. Finish me Billy, finish me," but Billy had shot his wad and he climbed off of her while she called him every dirty name she could think off. By that time the lot was almost empty and the help were starting to come out of the building and chase cars away so I started up and drove off. We dropped Sally off first and then Billy told me to drop him next.

"I ain't got to take her home and listen to her whine all the way," he said of Mary.

I dropped him off and we had no sooner pulled away from the front of his house than Bobby climbed over the seat and got in back with Mary. One block later he was fucking her and she was crying, "Get me off baby, get me off, make me cum." By the time I got to Bobby's place he had done the job and was sitting there with a smile on his face while Mary stayed on her back with a contented look on her face.

She was still lying on the back seat when we pulled away from Bobby's. When I stopped for the stop sign on the corner Mary sat up and asked, "Davy, are you still a virgin?" I hemmed and hawed and she said, "You can tell me Davy. It isn't a crime and all of us were at one time." I admitted that I still had my cherry and she said, "Would you like to fuck me Davy?" I didn't answer her – I was too tongue-tied – I was caught flat-footed by her question. "Of course you would. If you will do something for me Davy I'll let you fuck me. You can even fuck me twice because I know the first one will be pretty quick. Would you like to do that Davy? Would you like to fuck me tonight?"

I croaked out a yes and she told me where to drive and park.

"All you have to do to fuck me Davy, is eat my pussy."

"I can't do that."

"Why not?"

"Because Bobby and Billy have been there."

"Trust me Davy, it won't kill you and you might even like it."

"Oh man, that's gross."

"Oh come on Davy, it's your best chance to get rid of your virginity. Tell you what; you do it and I'll let you fuck me as many times as you can get it up. Come on baby, do Mary this favor. If you do a really nice job of it maybe we can go out on a couple of dates. Wouldn't you like that Davy? Wouldn't you like to date me and maybe fuck me?"

Well, I was desperate to get laid and so I let Mary talk me into climbing into the back seat with her. She instructed me in how she wanted it done and I was surprised when I did it and it didn't make me want to leap out of the car and heave in the bushes. I didn't really care for the taste, but what I did like was the way that Mary responded. She grabbed my head and pulled my face into her pussy and she went wild. She bucked, she pushed her muff up at me and she screamed – actually screamed – "Oh God yes Davy, don't stop, please God don't stop. Eat me you beautiful cunt licker, oh sweet Jesus you are good." She shook, she moaned, she made sharp little cries and her body seemed to spasm. I found out later that I had eaten her to an orgasm. When she was done she looked up at me with a look of wonder on her face and said, "It was really your first time? You really never ate pussy before?"

I told her no, that I was a virgin in all areas.

"You have a God given talent baby. No one has ever made me cum just by eating my pussy, no one! Oh baby, am I going to rock your world tonight."

My first time was embarrassingly quick, but my fist blowjob brought me back up in a hurry. My second time was a little better and my first sixty-nine got me my first taste of myself and another hard on. I fucked Mary three more times that night before she couldn't bring me to life again and she asked me to eat her after each time. When I dropped her at her house at oh dark thirty she spent five minutes kissing me good night and as she got out of the car she said, "You're mine from now on Davy. See you tonight after school."

I did see Mary after school the next day and so began one of the weirdest relationships I've ever seen. Mary and I became a somewhat steady couple. I say "somewhat" because Mary never gave up the other guys she was seeing. Mary was a slut. She had shown me that the night she took on both Billy and Bobby and Mary loved cock. Mary also loved the wicked feeling she got when she had me eat her pussy after another guy had fucked her. Maybe three nights a week she would go out with another guy and fuck him to death and when he dropped her off at home she would walk around to the alley behind her house where I would be waiting for her. She would squeal in delight as I cleaned her pussy out with my mouth and then she would fuck my eyes out until I couldn't get it up anymore. On the nights that she wasn't out with other guys she was with me

Everyone wondered why one of the most popular girls in the school spent so much time with me. Several of her girl friends even asked her what she saw, "In that dork." Mary never did give any of her friends the answer to that question and once I asked her why. "If I told them about your special talent baby I'd have to fight them all to keep them away from you."

"Is that all I am to you – a mouth?"

"Why baby, isn't it enough? Isn't what you have now 500% more than you had before I discovered what you can do?"

"Yeah but…"

"No buts baby. Face it, you aren't a real prize. You're a nice enough guy, but you are not all that attractive. Time will get rid of the pimples, but until you do something about your weight you won't be a catch for anyone, at least not anyone who doesn't know about your special talent. I'm seeing to it that you are one of the best fucked guys in school. Take what you have Davy and be happy for it."

She was right and I knew it, but it still hurt that she was so damned honest about it.

And then it was over. Mary received a scholarship to UCLA, but before she left for California she wanted one last night with me. Her parents were gone for the weekend and she asked me to stop by her house at eight. I got there to find Mary in the middle of a gangbang. She had seven guys there and as I watched they all took turns on her for three hours and that doesn't count what happened before I got there. About half an hour after I got there one of the guys said, "Come on Davy, it's your turn."

Mary said, "No, Davy gets his turn later. He is going to spend the night with me and I want him fresh."

That set up a chorus of "What's so special about him" and things were said like, "It sure ain't his cock. I've seen him in the locker room and he's nothing special." There were a lot more comments along those lines and then Mary said, "He is so special. He can make me scream and none of you guys have ever done that."

That got the guys going even more and I was starting to feel real uncomfortable and I was getting ready to split. Mary saw and knew what I was going to do.

"Davy, you don't have to if you don't want to, but please baby, one more time for me, please?"

I really didn't want to because I knew those guys and I knew what would happen, but the plea in Mary's voice made me say yes. I stripped and did what Mary loved more than anything else and she screamed and screamed her way through two orgasms and then she said, "Okay Davy baby, fuck me, fuck me hard and show them how it's done."

Either Mary was one great actress or there was something special about what was happening that night because she screamed and hollered as I fucked her and she bucked and bounced in a way that she hadn't for any of the others. When I was done she pushed me into a sixty-nine until I was hard and then she pulled me on top of her and we did it all over again. When I came the second time she said, "Let the others back in lover. I've got all night to take care of you."

The gangbang lasted until one in the morning and then Mary and I were alone. We fucked until I could not get it up anymore and Mary and I fell asleep in each other's arms. She left the following Monday and I never saw her again.

What I had known would happen happened. The guys who were at the gangbang spread the word about what I have done and pretty soon everyone was casting glances at me. The fallout was mixed, some good, some bad, some very good and some very, very bad. The worse was when some guys called me a closet queen, that I sucked cum out of a pussy because I was too scared to suck a cock. Other guys said that I was "one sick puppy" to have done what I did. The other side of the coin was the attention I got from the girls. I got more 'come ons' than I could believe, but I had a problem. Remember when I said I was inordinately shy? I got the come ons but I lacked the guts to make a move. After about a month one of the girls figured it out on her own and one day she came up to me and said, "Is what I've heard about you and Mary Koslowski true?" I nodded a yes. "I'm free tonight, are you?" From then on I had a steady stream of girl friends until I moved to Georgia to take a job.

Time did chase the pimples away and I finally did work up enough will power to lick my weight problem. I met and fell in love with Angie and we were married. We had three kids and lived your typical suburban life and things were perfect until Angie went to her class reunion. We couldn't get a baby sitter and so I had to stay home and watch the kids. Angie flew out on a Thursday and flew back home Sunday evening and when the kids and I picked her up at the airport I sensed something different about her. Nothing obvious, but something. That night she was eager to get to bed after we put the kids to bed and she was an absolute tiger. Our sex life has always been good, but that night it was great. Angie kept after me until I just could not answer the call again. As I lay next to her panting for breath I asked, "What got into you tonight? Did one of your old boyfriends get you all hot and horny at the reunion?"

"Something like that."

"I don't suppose you would care to expound on that?"

"Well, I did have a few cocks poked into my leg on the dance floor and I did get a few pretty heavy hits from some of my old beaus. I won't lie to you lover; I did get pretty close to giving it up to my old steady boyfriend – he's the one who got my cherry – but at the very last second I backed away. You might have never known, but then again you might have found out and I wasn't going to take a chance on losing you over a fling with an old boyfriend."

"That's it? You're horny because you almost got laid?"

"No sweetie, that isn't it. Does the name Mary Brenner ring a bell?"

"No, I can't say that it does."

How about her maiden name, Mary Koslowski?"

"Oh yes, I knew a Mary Koslowski."

"Pretty well from what I gathered."

"We going to dance around this or are you going to tell me what this is all about?"

"Did I ever mention Jerry Brenner?"

"Not that I recall."

"Jerry and I grew up next door to each other and we were in the same grade from second grade all the way through high school. When I got to the reunion I saw Jerry and there were empty seats at his table so I joined him. He introduced me to his wife Mary and when she heard my last name she said she used to date a Mitchell when she lived in Kansas City. I told her that you were from Kansas and she asked if your name was Davy by any chance. When I said that it was she laughed and commented on what a small world that it was. For the rest of the evening I got the feeling that she was watching me – appraising me in some way. It was after Todd, my old boyfriend, and I had returned from the dance floor after some hot and heavy petting that she said, "Do you do that often?"

"What?"

"Have other men and then take Davy home some desert?"

"I don't know what you are talking about."

"Oh well, maybe Davy has changed. It's nothing. Forget I even brought it up."

"Well you know me sweetie, wave something like that in front of me and I'm after it like a dog after a bone. I waited until she went to the bathroom and I followed her. We were alone and so I kept pushing at her until she told me about what the two of you used to do. She saw the way

I was acting with Todd and she just knew I was going to fuck him and she had wondered if I did it often and then took the cream pie home to you. Did you really eat her pussy after other guys had used her?"

"I'm afraid so," I said and then I told Angie the story of how it got started.

"She said you could actually make her scream."

"Yeah, well, Mary was different. Her greatest turn on was for me to eat her after she'd been out playing with someone else. I'm not so sure that it was anything that I did that made her scream as much as it was the idea of what I was doing."

"Did you really do it after a gangbang?"

"Yeah. It was the last time, just before she left for UCLA."

"How come I never knew that about you?"

"Because you are not a slut my love, and also for the same reason I didn't know that it was a Todd that took your cherry. You and I have never talked about what we did before we got married. I wonder if marriage has changed Mary any."

"In what way?"

"She was a slut honey. Anyone, anytime, anyplace and she wasn't all that particular when it came to how many guys were there. I wonder if she has changed and if not, what kind of relationship she might have with this Jerry."

"Why?"

"No reason, just curious. But that aside, what was it about Mary and your talk with her that made you such a sexual dynamo tonight?"

"You won't laugh or get pissed at me?"

"No, of course not."

"The picture of you at a gangbang eating her pussy after all those guys had her just lit me off."

"You can't be serious."

"Oh but I am sweetie. Just the thought of you eating her pussy after someone else fucked her drove me wild."

"Why? I eat your pussy after we have made love and that's the same thing."

"No it isn't sweetie, not by a long shot. That's just you in there, not seven other guys and that's the thought that turned me on."

Things changed after that, at least as far as our sex life was concerned. We went from two or three nights a week to five or six and where I only used to eat Angie's pussy after we made love occasionally now she wanted me to do it all the time. Hey, I like my sex as much as the next guy so I was going to complain? Not hardly, but I'm not stupid; I knew what was going on. Angie was imagining Mary and me and it was turning her on. I suppose I should have given more thought to it than I did, but I didn't. I thought she would get over it in time, but after three months Angie was still going strong.

And then suddenly, virtually overnight, Angie turned moody on me. Tuesday night she fucked me like a woman possessed, but on Wednesday she pushed me away. Thursday we made love, but it wasn't the frenzied coupling of the previous three months. We went back to having sex twice a week, but only once a night instead of the three or four we had been doing and she wouldn't let me eat her pussy anymore. She became quiet around me and once in a while I would catch her looking at me and as soon as our eyes would meet she would avert her gaze. This went on for a couple of weeks and I don't know how much longer it might have gone on had I not come home from work an hour early one day to find her lying on our bed and crying. I sat down on the bed next to her and asked her what was wrong as I reached out and touched her face. She gave a loud sob and turned away from me.

"I don't want to talk about it."

"You have to Angie. Something has been bothering you for weeks now and it is affecting our relationship and I want to know what it is. We can't fix it if I don't know what is wrong."

"It can't be fixed. It is too late for that."

"Nonsense baby, anything can be fixed."

"Not now. Not now Davy. We can talk later when I'm not so weepy."

"Okay Angie, but I'm going to hold you to it. I'll expect you to talk to me before we go to bed tonight."

I went downstairs and started dinner. Angie didn't come down so I fixed her a plate and put it in the microwave and then I did the dinner dishes. I helped the kids with their homework, watched some TV with them and then put them to bed. I sat down on the couch and started watching CNN and I was watching some twit babble about the prospects for peace in the middle east when Angie came into the room. She sat down in the easy chair across from the couch which in itself was not a good sign since she had always preferred to sit next to me because she liked to touch and be touched while we read, watched TV or talked. I picked up the remote and shut off the TV and waited.

She was red-eyed from crying and she kept glancing nervously around the room – anything to keep from having to meet my eyes. Finally I broke the silence, "Whatever it is Angie, it can't be so bad that we can't do something about it. Just spit it out and get it over with."

She looked down at the floor, took a deep breath and then still looking away from me she said, "It can't be fixed Davy. I've been stupid, totally stupid and I've ruined my life and maybe yours. I've trashed our marriage. I've taken everything good that we had and I've shit all over it because of a dumb, crazy obsession."

"Oh come on Angie, it can't be that bad."

"Oh yes it can Davy. I've lied to you, I've deceived you and I've cheated on you, and all because of a stupid, stupid fantasy."

I sat there, totally stunned by what Angie had just said. Angie had cheated on me? That was inconceivably, just totally inconceivable. I started to say something, but Angie cut me off.

"Just let me get it out Davy, then you can call me a whore and throw me out, but let me get this over with first."

It had started with her class reunion and her talk with Mary Brenner. She had come home with the image of me sucking the cum of other men out of Mary and that image was a super turn on for her. The more she thought about it the hotter she got and the more she wanted sex. Gradually the image changed from Mary and me to Angie and me. Angie began to fantasize about me eating her pussy after some other man had fucked her. Over the next month or so the fantasy grew from me eating one man out of her to my eating two. Then it was three, four and finally the seven men from a gangbang. The fantasy was so strong and powerful that Angie was fucking herself with a dildo while she waited for me to get home.

On Tuesday nights Angie plays bridge with several of her girlfriends and one night one of the girls asked Angie to give her a ride to the bar where she was supposed to meet her boyfriend. Angie went inside to have a drink with Becky and she was introduced to Becky's boyfriend Harry. Harry had a friend with him and Angie's one drink turned into several and when Harry's friend asked her to dance she had gotten up and moved out onto the dance floor with him. She wasn't surprised when she felt his erection poke into her leg, but she had been surprised at the thought that had entered her mind. She could fuck him and then come home to me and actually see what it would be like to have me suck another man's cum out of her. As fast as the idea had entered her mind she had chased it away. But a couple of more drinks and a couple of more dances and the thought was back.

She had excused herself to go to the bathroom and Becky got up to go with her.

"He thinks you're hot," Becky said.

"What?"

"Jim. He thinks you're hot. He'd fuck you if you gave him a chance."

"You can't be serious."

Oh yes I am. Your back seat, his back seat, a motel room – he would do you in a heartbeat."

"Honestly Becky, I'm a happily married woman and I don't run around on Dave. Besides, Jim is just a baby. He's what, twenty-five or so? I'm a thirty-eight year old woman."

"You are a hot looking woman sweetie and age has nothing to do with it. He's yours if you want him."

Two more drinks, another dance and Angie was in Jim's car on the back seat with her legs kicking in the air as Jim pounded his cock into her.

"As soon as it was over guilt took charge and all the way home I cursed myself for being a stupid fool, but the closer I got to home the more I thought that I had another man's cum in me and I would soon be home and you and I would go to bed and make love and then you would eat me. I got all tingly when I thought that and by the time I was in the house I was so hot that I would have fucked a parking lot full of Jims. I climbed into bed with you and the sex was so intense and satisfying that I didn't think of anything else. Then, after we had both climaxed, I started to panic. What if you could tell when you tasted me? I was going to get up and run for the bathroom, but you were too quick for me and as soon as your tongue touched me the panic fled and I had another orgasm. At that point I didn't care if you would know or not, all I wanted was for you to eat my pussy and suck Jim's leavings out of me. I had three orgasms while you lapped up his sperm, each more intense that the last. I didn't start to feel guilty again until after you fell asleep and then I lay awake all night with my thoughts alternating between guilt and the pleasure that I had just enjoyed. I spent the rest of the week swearing that I would never, ever do anything that stupid again."

The next Tuesday I again drove Becky over to the bar. Jim was there with Harry and that night we didn't waste any time on drinks or dancing. Ten minutes after I got there I was on my back on his back seat and he sent me home to you with four loads of his juice in my pussy. You fucked me and then ate me and I came so many times that night that I fell asleep totally exhausted. I woke up in the morning ashamed of myself and feeling intense guilt over what I was having you do and I promised myself that it would never happen again, but the next Tuesday I was at the bar and in Jim's car again. He fucked me three times and then got up to go back into the bar and use the bathroom. I was lying there on the back seat with my eyes closed finger fucking myself and dreaming about the way I was going to feel when I got home to you when Jim came back and slid his cock in only it wasn't Jim. Harry and Becky had had a fight and Becky had caught a cab home. Harry was already in me and pounding away so there wasn't much I could do about it. Half way through his fucking me I thought about your first time with Mary and how you had eaten her after the two boys had fucked her and I stared to get hot thinking about how I was going to be able to experience the same thing. Between Jim and Harry I had seven loads of cum in me when I came home that night and I was going crazy between thinking how intense the sex was going to be and how I couldn't possibly get what I had done past you. I panicked when you commented on how wet I was and I was surprised as hell when you accepted my explanation that I was so wet because I had been hot for you all day. My orgasms that night were so strong that I almost passed out. The next morning I was so guilt ridden that I couldn't hold food down and I wretched all day and swore to God that I would put an end to what I was doing.

"But as the days went by and I thought about how it felt to have so many mind-blowing orgasms my resolve slipped and the following Tuesday I skipped bridge and met Jim and Harry at a motel and the two of them fucked me for five hours. The sex with you that night was everything that I had hoped for, but I was still so keyed up that I had to use my dildo on myself after you fell asleep. The next day the guilt was back in spades and everything I ate for the next three days I tossed up. I wasn't able to eat, I couldn't sleep, I was an absolute mess, but by Friday I was looking forward to Tuesday. Tuesday I skipped bridge again and met Jim and Harry at the motel only that time they had a friend with them and then the Tuesday after that it was two friends and then it was four and then five.

"I can't explain it Davy, I honestly can't explain what came over me. It had nothing to do with my love for you; you are still my whole world. It was all me. I couldn't have cared less about those dickheads that were fucking me. They were all of them just a means to an end. All I thought about was what you did with Mary and how I wanted to experience the same things. I don't know, maybe I thought that she had a part of you and that I needed to take back from her and the only way to do it was outdo her. Three weeks ago I got to the motel and found nine men waiting for me. I took one look and then I turned and ran. Since then I have stayed home and tried to be a good wife to you, but I'm dying inside. Sure, I've lived my fantasy, but at the cost of my self respect. I've blown my wedding vows all to hell and the worst of it is that I used you. I let you suck the cum of strangers out of me with no thought other than my own sexual gratification. Don't misunderstand me here Dave, when I was in bed with you I was making love to you, not fucking, it is just that...shit! I don't know what it was. It was part fantasy and part wanting to have as much of you as Mary had. What I ended up being was what you called her – a slut! I'm a fucking whore

Dave and it is killing me to know that I did it to myself and that I've ruined my life. I hope I haven't ruined yours Dave. I know you'll hate me now, but believe me Dave, you can't possibly hate me more than I hate myself."

She started crying again and she got up and ran back up to the bedroom.

I wish I could say that I ran up the stairs after her, took her in my arms and told her that I still loved her, and that everything would be all right, but I can't. I couldn't bring myself to even touch her after that and after a month of drifting farther and farther apart I packed up and moved out. I've seen a lawyer and the divorce is in the works. When I pick the kids up on the weekends Angie stays out of sight. The kids don't understand what's going on and they are too young for me to tell them and even if I could, how could I make them understand when I don't understand it myself.

End of the 4th Story

Frank and Diane

The day showed no signs of being a disaster when I woke up. The alarm went off at five and my wife Diane reached for me and pulled me back down as I started to get out of bed. She kissed me, slipped me a little tongue and her hand reached for my cock. Twenty-five years and the woman could still turn me into a quivering wreck. She pulled me on top of her and as my cock parted her nether lips she said:

"Make it a good morning lover; make it a very good morning."

I pushed into her and she moaned, "Oh God yes lover, do it hard lover, do it."

She moaned, she cried, she dug her nails into the cheeks of my ass and pulled me to her and then she came just seconds before I did.

She got up to fix the coffee while I took my showered and then I fixed us breakfast while she showered. We discussed what our days were likely to be like as we ate and then she asked:

"Meatloaf and baked potatoes okay for dinner tonight?"

"Sounds great. I'll stop at the bakery and pick up a loaf of fresh French bread and maybe a pecan pie."

"Ooooh, pecan pie. Out to spoil me are you?"

"Can't think of anyone I'd rather spoil."

We kissed and walked hand in hand into the garage, kissed once more and then we both headed off to work.

***

The drive in was uneventful and so was the first half of the morning. Around eleven Harry (my boss) called me into his office.

"We have a situation in St. Louis. Baker caught Smithers with his wife and now Baker is in jail and Smithers is in the hospital. There is no one there to run the office. I hate to do this to you on such short notice, but you have to catch the two-twenty flight, get to St. Louis and take charge of the office.

"I don't know how long you will be there. I guess it will depend on just how bad Baker fucked up Smithers. If it is too bad he might not get out of jail for a while and Smithers might not get out of the hospital anytime soon. Even if the both get out soon I don't see how they will be able to work together. I'll have to think long and hard on it, but I can't see anyway other than to let one of them go. Which one I don't know. I'll need a lot more information before I can make that decision."

"Seems cut and dried to me. Smithers fucked with Baker's wife. Smithers should have expected Baker to get pissed if he ever found out."

"I don't know for a fact that Baker caught Smithers with his wife or that Smithers is even guilty. All I've got is what the secretary told me when she called. Maybe you can find out more for me when you get there."

I called Diane to let her know what was going on, but her secretary told me that she was in a meeting. I told her I'd call back and then I headed home to pack a bag.

Diane's car was in the driveway when I got home and I wondered what was up with that. She was supposed to be in a meeting. When I walked into the living room I saw that she was indeed in a meeting, but it wasn't the kind of meeting I had envisioned when her secretary told me she was in one.

There was a trail of clothing on the floor leading from the couch to the stairway and some of those clothes were men's clothes. At the foot of the steps there was a pair of men's trousers and I picked them up and found a wallet in one of the back pockets. I took it out, opened it up and read the name Stanton North on the driver's license. I put the wallet in my pocket and then looked around the room and saw a suit coat over the back of the easy chair. It yielded a checkbook and I put that in my pocket too.

I walked up the stairs and as I got close to the top of the steps I began hearing what was coming from the bedroom.

"Fuck me. Fuck me hard."

"Like it do you?"

"Oh God yes. You feel so good in me. Fuck me baby, fuck me."

"I would never have believed you could be such a hot little slut. Like my cock?"

"Love your cock. Just keep giving it to me."

I walked into the room and saw a man pounding into Diane and she had her legs wrapped around him and her hands on his ass pulling him to her.

"Fuck me, fuck me, fuck me" she was moaning as I walked past on my way to the closet. I was almost to the closet door before Stanton North saw me and he stopped in mid-stroke and said:

"Oh shit!"

Diane had her eyes closed as he fucked her and when he stopped they popped open and she cried:

"Don't stop. Damn it, don't stop, I'm almost th…" and then she saw me and cried "No. Oh God no" and started trying to get out from under North.

"Don't stop on my account," I said as I entered the closet. "I just need to pack a bag and then I'll get out of here and leave you two love birds alone."

I had my back to them as I took socks and underwear out of the dresser drawer and put them in the suitcase, but I could hear them behind me. Diane was saying "Get off me damn it" while North was saying "Christ what a mess." When I turned to go back into the closet for a garment bag I saw North heading out the bedroom door and Diane scrambling to find something to cover herself with. As she scrambled she was saying things like:

"What are you doing Frank? Why are you packing" and uttering nonsense like "It isn't what you think Frank" and "I can explain Frank."

While she was babbling I heard the front door slam shut and I wondered where North was going. Diane's car was the only one in the driveway so he must have arrived with her.

I ignored Diane as I finished packing and I didn't respond to her "We need to talk Frank. You have to let me explain."

I walked out the front door without having said a word since walking into the bedroom and telling them not to stop on my account. As I walked to my car Diane was hollering:

"Wait Frank; don't go. Please talk to me."

As I opened my car door I looked around but saw no sign of Stanton North. Maybe he was hiding somewhere watching and would come back when he saw me drive away. Diane was running down the front walk and almost had her hand on the passenger side door handle when I pulled away from the curb.

It is an absolute wonder that I made it to the airport without killing myself or someone else. My mind was definitely not on my driving. How had it happened? Why had it happened? I would have bet all that I had that Diane and I were rock solid. I looked back on our life together and I didn't see anything – not one thing – that would ever have led me to believe that what I had just seen was even remotely possible. My God! How could she have done what she did to me when we got up that morning and then do what I had just seen her doing?

***

Diane and I met when my father received a promotion and had to move the family fifteen hundred miles away. The move was a bitch as far as I was concerned. I was taken away from the kids I had grown up with and gone to school with and then dumped into a school where I didn't know a single soul. I was sitting alone at a table in the school cafeteria at lunch time and feeling sorry for myself when the most beautiful girl I had ever seen came over to the table and sat down with me. She set her tray down and said:

"Hi there new kid."

She reached across the table and stuck out her hand and said. "I'm Diane." It took me a second or two before I realized she was offering me her hand to shake. I took it and said:

"Hi Diane, I'm Frank."

"Where you from Frank?" she asked and then we spent the rest of the lunch period getting to know each other. She had joined me at my table because she had known what I was going through because the same thing had happened to her the previous year. By the time the bell rang we had made a date for her to show me around the town.

Within six weeks we were going steady and like all typical teenagers we were making out like mad. Being a guy with raging hormones I naturally tried to get Diane to go all the way, but she wouldn't do it. She was determined to honor her promise to her mother to go to her marriage bed a virgin. Luckily for my sanity she broke that promise on her eighteenth birthday.

We had some serious discussions after the night she gave me her cherry. I told her that I wanted to marry her, but that I didn't want to get married until I finished college. She wanted to get married right away and she wasn't happy with me because I wanted to wait. I was telling my mom about it when she surprised the hell out of me. I'd always thought of my mom as being a bit on the prudish side, but she said:

"So move in with her and live together until you graduate."

"How can I do that? The reason I want to wait is so that I can afford it. No way I can support a wife and go to school at the same time."

"You might have to get a part time job to help out with the groceries, but your college fund has enough in it to let you rent a small place off campus."

I thought about it and then brought it up to Diane. We talked it over and decided we would both get part time jobs and do it. We went looking and found a small apartment that I could afford and then we went to do the hard part – tell her parents.

Her mom was horrified that Diane hadn't kept to her promise on holding on to her virginity. She cried and blubbered while Diane's father called me every name in the book and some that he made up on the spot. Then he told Diane that he absolutely forbid it and furthermore she was never to see me again. Diane looked at me and asked me to wait in the car. Ten minutes later she came out carrying two suitcases.

She never told me what went on when I left the house, but it was three years before she ever talked to her parents again and only then to tell them that they had a grandson. Suddenly I was a great guy, their daughter was lucky to have found me and on and on and on. But the damage had already been done and on my part I tolerated them, but that was all. Diane eventually forgave them and they became part of our lives. They were great grandparents to our three kids, but like I said, I just tolerated them.

The years passed by, the kids grew up and set out on their own and now this. At least the kids wouldn't grow up having divorced parents.

***

I got to the airport early, checked in and then sat down in one of the many airport coffee shops to wait for my flight to be called. I took out North's wallet and checkbook and began going through them. Behind his driver's license I found a card the said "Emergency Information." It gave his blood type and some other information, but the part that caught my eye was the part where it gave his emergency contact. Arlis North and under "Relationship" it said "wife" and it gave a number where she could be reached. I took out my cell phone and called it.

"Hello?"

"Mrs. North?"

"Yes."

"My name is Frank Bellows. I'm sorry to be making this call, but I just found your husband in bed with my wife and I thought you should know."

"You're joking, right?"

"No ma'am, I'm afraid not."

"Well I don't believe you Mr. Whoever you are. My Stan would never do a thing like that to me."

"Tell you what. When he gets home tonight ask him if he knows a Diane Bellows and then ask him to show you his wallet and checkbook. He won't be able to because I have them. I took them out of his clothes when I found them lying on my living room floor when I went home early. I am at the airport right now waiting to catch a flight to St. Louis. When I get back home I'd be happy to hand deliver them to you."

"You are really serious about this?"

"I'm sorry, but I am."

"When will you be back?"

"I don't know. I have to go and fill in for someone who is off sick and I'll be there until he can get back to work."

"Could you mail me the wallet and checkbook?"

"I could I suppose, but I'll let you know this ahead of time. Your husband's wallet has eighty-seven dollars in it and after what I saw when I walked into my bedroom I feel a crying need to get drunk and drown my sorrows and your hubby is going to foot the bill for it. There will probably be some left, but I have no idea how much."

"Send it to my office." She gave me the address and I wrote it down and then she said, "If you can send it overnight and I'll reimburse you."

"I can do that. They just called my flight so I have to go."

I said goodbye and disconnected. North got lucky. My original plan was to leave his wallet and credit cards on the counter in the bathroom and hope that whoever found it would go on a spending spree, but getting in touch with his wife changed all that. Hopefully she would make his life a living hell.

My cell had been going off almost from the moment I left the house and every time I looked it was Diane so I didn't take the call. It rang again as I was leaving the coffee shop and I looked expecting it to be another call from Diane, but this time it was from the office. I called back and got Harry.

"You need to call home Frank. Diane just called me and she is frantic because she can't get in touch with you."

"There is a reason for that Harry. I'm not taking her calls. When I went home to pack she was there and she wasn't alone and she was doing things she shouldn't have been doing. I'll talk with her when I get back. Maybe by then I'll have calmed down enough not to wrap my hands around her throat and squeeze. Make things easy on yourself and tell the receptionist not to take her calls."

***

The first thing I did after seeing to it that the office was running smoothly and that there were no immediate problems was to hit the Post Office and send Mrs. North her husband's wallet and checkbook. I included the information on where I was staying so she could call if she had any questions. That taken care of I called the police and found out where Baker was being held and if I could see him.

Outside of bruised knuckles and a broken finger Baker didn't look too bad. He hadn't had a bail hearing yet because the powers that be were waiting on word from the hospital on just how bad Smithers was so they would know what charges to file. I told him about Harry's concerns and asked him for the story.

It sounded all too familiar.

He had returned home during his lunch hour to pick up something that he had forgotten to take with him in the morning and he'd walked in on Smithers who was using his lunch hour to pork Baker's wife. While he was stomping the shit out of Smithers his wife was on the phone to 911 telling them that her husband had gone crazy and that she feared for her life. The cops showed up, Smithers went to the hospital and Baker went to jail.

My next stop was to the hospital to see Smithers. He had a broken nose, two broken ribs, two cracked ribs and they had removed his right testicle. From him I got:

"It wasn't my fault. The bitch came after me so of course I tapped her. I'm single and I like pussy as much as the next guy. If anybody is at fault here it is Baker. If he took care of the bitch and gave her what she needed she wouldn't be out looking."

He got no sympathy from me. I called Harry and told him the story and said that my recommendation was to transfer Smithers out of the office unless he could find some grounds for firing the guy and I told him I would take a hard look at things in the office and see if I could find something that he could use.

Baker's hearing was the next day and bail was set at two hundred and fifty thousand. The only way he could come up with the money was to put his house up as collateral, but his wife refused to sign off on it so he was going to have to sit in jail until his father and brother could arrange something.

The next morning at nine-thirty I got a call from Arlis North. She told me that when her husband came home she asked him if he knew a Diane Bellows and she said that his face lost all of its color as he said that he didn't know a Diane Bellows. She asked him if he was sure and he said that he was pretty sure. Then she asked him for his wallet and checkbook and he patted his pockets and said that he must have left them on his desk at work.

"Then he changed the subject and asked what was for dinner. He knows he is in deep shit, but he doesn't know how deep it is and he won't know until tomorrow when I ask him for his wallet and checkbook again. Do you have any idea of how long it was going on?"

"I just know that it was. I walked in on them and then I left."

"What does your wife have to say?"

"No idea. I haven't spoken to her since walking into the bedroom and catching them and I won't be talking to her until I get home."

"When you do talk to her call me. I'd like to compare their stories."

"Will do. I'd like to hear both sides too."

***

I had a dozen calls a day from Diane, but I didn't take any of them. Harry must have told her I was in St. Louis and she must have gotten the office number from information. Dixie, our receptionist, told me that I had a call on line three and when I picked it up it was Diane.

"What do you want Diane?"

"We need to talk Frank. I need to explain that what happened isn't what you think."

"I'm in no mood to talk to you right now. I'm still at the point where I want to strangle you to death and then take my shotgun and go looking for your lover and kill him too."

"He is not my lov….."

"Save it Diane. Don't call here anymore. We will talk when I get home and not before" and I hung up on her.

In mid-afternoon I got a call from Baker's father telling me that bail had been arranged and that he would be released the next morning. In a way I was sorry to hear that. As long as Baker was in jail and

Smithers was in the hospital I didn't have to go home and deal with Diane.

I had dinner and drinks on North again that night and made it back to my room about seven. The phone rang and since only Harry and Arlis North had the number I answered it. It was Arlis. We exchanged hellos and then she filled me in on the latest from her end.

"When he got home I asked him again for his wallet and checkbook and he said that they were gone from his office when he got there. He said that someone on the night cleaning crew must have taken them and that he would file a complaint when he went in to work the next morning."

I had to laugh at that. "Just how long does he think he can put it off?"

"I don't know how long he thought he could, but I put an end to it. I asked him just how stupid that he thought I was. I told him that he knew he was busted when I asked about your wife and then asked for the wallet and checkbook. There was only one way I could have put the two of them together and he knew it. Then the dumb shit said that he didn't know what I was talking about. That pissed me off so I took his wallet and checkbook out of my purse and threw them in his face. Then I told him how I'd gotten them and that I'd called his office and found out that he worked with the woman he claimed he didn't know. Then I fibbed a bit. I told him that when you got home from St. Louis you were going to stop by and show me the pictures you took with your cell phone camera before they knew you were there."

"How did he take that?"

"He finally realized that he was caught and he broke down, begged forgiveness and swore that it was the only time that he had ever been unfaithful. He said he couldn't help it, that your wife had chased him for months and that it was hard to ignore a beautiful woman who was hot for your body."

"Too bad I wasn't thinking a little more clearly when I walked in on them. My cell phone does have a camera; I just never thought to use it. Do you believe his story?"

"That she chased after him? It could be true. She wouldn't be the first. Was it only the one time with her? That could be true too, but he was lying through his teeth when he said that it was the only time he ever cheated. I know of at least three times that he has strayed. Well, that's not quite true. Three times I've had people tell me that he ran around on me when I was out of town visiting relatives. I've never confronted him on them, because I really didn't want to know if it was true."

"You said that his saying that Diane chased him could be true and that she wouldn't have been the first. Why did you say that?"

"Stan is rather well endowed and some women when they hear that want to check it out."

"A week ago I would have said Diane would never do anything like that, but that was before I walked in on her and your husband."

"I've got to go, but if I learn anything else I'll give you a call. Don't forget; I want to her hear side when you get home and talk with her."

"I won't."

***

At eleven the next morning Ray Baker called me to let me know he was out of jail on bail. He was going to have to take the rest of the day and the next day to take care of personal business. His wife had taken out a restraining order on him and he needed to find a place to stay and make arrangements with the court to get into his house to get his personal things. He said that he would be in on Thursday.

I called Harry and brought him up to date and then I told him that in checking into things at the office I had found that Smithers had been fudging his expense reports and that could possibly be grounds for letting him go. I told him I would probably fly home Thursday evening and that I was going to need to take Friday off to handle my personal affairs and I would see him Monday morning.

I managed to get through the next two days without incident and on Thursday morning Ray was back at work. I brought him up to date on what was going on in the office and then because I was going through something similar I asked him how things were going on the home front.

"The restraining order only keeps me five hundred feet away from her. I can access the house whenever I want as long as she isn't there. If she is there and won't leave when I want to go in I have to get someone from the court to go in with me. I just waited down the street until she went to work and then me and my brother went in and got everything that I wanted. I have no need to go back.

"I don't know what the stupid cunt is thinking. She got the order, but that was all. She didn't touch the bank accounts. I cleaned them out yesterday."

"I thought that this was a no fault state and that everything had to be split fifty-fifty."

"In a divorce that would be true, but I'm not talking divorce; I'm just walking away. If she wants a divorce she can pay for it and when she files she will be entitled to fifty percent of our assets at the time she files and that will be zip. We took out a second on the house to finish the basement and make it into a recreation room so there is no equity in the house and the money I took out of the bank will be long gone. I can claim that I needed it all to set me up in a new place when she barred me from the house. That reminds me. I need to call Harry and get my insurance and all of that other crap changed."

"She tell you why she did it?"

"I haven't spoken to the whore since the cops hauled me away and I have no intention of talking to her. It doesn't matter why she did it; it only matters that she did."

I decided to get a good night's sleep before going home and having to talk to Diane so I called the airline and made reservations for the morning flight.

***

I was rested when I got up and I had a good breakfast before catching the airport shuttle and I was home in Denver by eleven. I hit the bank, cleaned out the savings, cashed in five of the nine certificates of deposit in the deposit box and put all the money in the checking account.

Diane was at work when I got home so I would be alone until six. I got on the phone, got pay off balances for all of our credit cards and then cancelled all but five of them. I kept the American Express card that I used primarily for business expenses and two of the other cards in my name and put two in Diane's name. I went back to the bank and arranged wire transfers to pay off the cards using the money in the checking account. That done I took half of the money left in checking and opened a checking account in my name only. I arranged for another safe deposit box in my name only and put two of the remaining four CDs into it and then went back home.

When the kids had grown and moved out I had converted one of their bedrooms into a home office and den and the other two were kept as spare rooms for when the kids came home to visit. I picked the spare bedroom next to the den and moved all of my things into it. I was all moved in and set up when Diane came home.

I heard Diane come in and call for me. "Frank? Frank? Where are you?"

I ignored her as I heard her walking through the house looking for me. She finally came upstairs and I had my back to the door when she came in.

"Frank? I ignored her. "Frank? Please Frank; we need to talk."

I turned to face her. "Where is it written that I have to talk to an unfaithful whore?" She winced when I said that and then I said, "However we do need to talk about finances."

"Finances? Why?"

"Because your actions have made changes necessary. Go on downstairs and take a seat at the kitchen table and I'll be down in a minute."

She left and I sorted through the papers I had been working on, picked up the ones I needed and then followed Diane down to the kitchen and took a seat across from her.

"While I was gone I had a lot of time to think about what I should do and in the end I decided to do nothing."

I saw relief on her face when I said that, but it faded when I said, "By nothing I mean that I will be having little or nothing to do with you. I can't see wasting money on divorce attorneys especially since at my age I don't see another marriage in my future so I'm not going to need single status. If you want a divorce you can go for it and pay for it. For now though there are some changes."

I explained all that I had done with the credit cards, the savings, the CDs and the checking account. "You can have the original deposit box, but I would recommend that you open your own checking and savings accounts and we will leave the old joint account in place and call it the household account. With me so far?"

"But why are you do…"

"You know damned well why Diane. Okay now, the household account will be used for household expenses." I slid a piece of paper across the table to her. "That is a list of what it takes to run the house. House payment, electric bill, phone, gas, water and sewage, taxes and insurance. What we are from now on is roommates. You will need to deposit half of the amount on that paper into the household account every month from now on. We will share the house with the exception of two rooms. You will have the master bedroom as your room and Carol's old room will be my bedroom."

"Why are you moving into Carol's room? You need to be in the master bedroom with me."

"After what I saw taking place in that room? There is no way I'm going to stay in that room, sleep on that bed or have anything to do with the woman I saw doing what she was doing on that bed."

"That's what we need to talk about Frank. What you saw isn't what you think."

"Of course it was what I think it was. It was you fucking another man in our house and on our bed."

"Okay Frank, but what you need to understand is that is all that it was – fucking. There was no love or affection involved; it was just me satisfying my curiosity. I love you Frank. I always have and I always will. What I felt for Stan was just a little bit of lust and that's all. It was a one-time thing to satisfy my curiosity and if you had not have come home you would never have known and it would have never happened again."

"But that is the problem Diane. I did come home and I do know and because I know it changes everything. You cheated on me and that means that you can't be trusted. If you can't be trusted that means that everything you say has to be weighed and looked at to try and determine if it is the truth or a lie. You say you love me. Can you love me and still betray me? Can you love me and still disrespect me by bringing another man into my house and then fucking him on my bed? The same bed you would have slept on with me that night? How much love and respect would you be showing me by giving me that man's leavings if I would have made love to you that night?

"No Diane, you can no longer be trusted. You say it was a one time thing and would have never happened again. Truth or lie? I only have your word for it that it is true, but you can't be trusted. It could just as easily been the tenth time and you could have already set up a time to do it again. But, and this is the part that counts, even if it is the truth you still stabbed me in the back. You broke the promise that you made to me when we took our vows and for what? To satisfy some curiosity of yours? Just what the hell were you so curious about that you were willing to risk your marriage to satisfy it?"

She looked away from me when she said, "The size of his penis."

"You have got to be shitting me. The size of his dick? Why in the hell were you curious about the size of his dick?"

"Some of the girls in the office had gone out with him and they raved about how big it was and how filling it was. I listened to all the stories they told, but I didn't pay a whole lot of attention to them until he started hitting on me. Even then it was a while before I started thinking about it."

"You are saying that he tried to seduce you?"

"I guess he was, but I didn't pay a whole lot of attention to it at first. But I liked the attention and what woman doesn't like to feel that she is attractive. At my age it was a hell of a boost to my self-esteem to have a man ten years younger than me to paying attention to me. I had lunch with him a couple of times and danced with him a couple of times when everyone in the office would stop for drinks. It was dancing with him that started me thinking of the stories I'd heard about him. I felt him push against me a time or two and he did seem rather large.

"The more I thought about the stories the more curious I got. I was a virgin when I met you and you are the only man I've ever known sexually. I got to wondering what another man would be like especially a man reputed to be as big as Stan. He kept working on me and I kept wondering and I finally let my curiosity get the best of me."

"You say all the other girls talked about Stan's size and abilities in bed? How many other girls?"

"Seven of them."

"Stan had sex with seven of them?"

"They said he did."

"Seven of them in your office alone. That would seem to show that Stan was pretty promiscuous. Did you ever stop to think that a guy who was fucking anything that moved might pick up a disease or two somewhere along the line?"

"Oh come on Frank. If that were the case he would have given it to the girls he made love to and you can believe that if he did it would be broadcast all over the office in minutes."

"You can have it and not know it Diane. In some cases you can have it for months before you show signs. If I were you I'd go and get myself tested."

"The important thing Frank is that Stan meant nothing to me. There was no love involved and I can't say that there was even much like."

"That's not what it sounded like when I walked into the room."

"You know I like sex Frank and you know how vocal I get when I make love to you. So I made some noise. It was because I was in the middle of having sex and not because I had any special feelings for Stan. It was a mistake Frank. A major mistake and I'm sorry as hell that I slipped up and I can promise you that it will never happen again. I love you Frank and you know that I do. You can't throw away twenty-five good years because of one mistake."

"I'm not throwing anything away Diane. You are the one who threw it away when you brought another man into my house and took him on my bed."

I got up and left the kitchen and went back upstairs to the den and lost myself in some paperwork.

***

I'm a fairly light sleeper and that night about an hour after I went to bed the noise of the bedroom door opening woke me up. Diane quietly moved into the room and softly closed the door behind her. I sleep nude and it was summer so I was lying on top of the covers. Diane bent over me and took my cock into her mouth. She had always been able to turn me to jelly when she blew me and it looked like she planned to do it again in an attempt to get back into my good graces. She was totally surprised when I pushed her away.

"Leave me alone Diane. I am not in the least bit interested in North's leftovers."

She got off the bed and left the room crying. Maybe twenty minutes later I fell asleep and I wasn't bothered the rest of the night.

Diane was in the kitchen making coffee when I came down from taking my morning shower and getting ready to go to work. Her "Good morning Frank" was met with a noncommittal grunt. I ignored her until the coffee was ready and then filled my travel mug and left for work. I waited until ten before calling Arlis North and then I filled her in on what I'd found out.

"Seven other girls?"

"That is what she said. Apparently your husband was the office Romeo."

"Do you believe her story?"

"Before I walked in on her and your husband I would have believed her if she had told me that the sun was now rising in the west, but after? I don't know. It could be true or it could be that she is just trying to put a better light on what she did by making me think that it really meant nothing. I mean how do you know? When she got caught trust went out the window. Everything she says now has to be seen as self serving."

"Have you decided what you are going to do?"

"The marriage is dead, but if there is a divorce she will have to be the one to go for it. My plan right now is to simply cohabit. We will coexist as roommates, but that is all. I can't see ruining myself financially just because she couldn't keep her panties on. How about you? Got a plan yet?"

"I'm still thinking on it. Keep in touch Frank."

"Will do Arlis. Good luck."

***

For the next week I made sure that I was up and gone before Diane woke up and I found things to do that kept me from going home until late. Diane was usually up waiting for me, but I ignored her. The next weekend she tried to slip into my bed again, but I told her to get away from me and leave me alone.

"Damn it Frank; don't do this to me. I love you Frank and I want you."

"I don't want you Diane. You are damaged goods."

"My God Frank. It was only once. I haven't even talked to him since he ran out of the house. It was a one time slip in judgment Frank. Please! Give me a chance. I know it was wrong and I'm sorry. I swear to God that it will never happen again."

"The problem Diane is that I don't know that it was only once. He may have been your third or fourth lover or your tenth. You may still be doing him on your lunch hours in a motel. When I caught you with him you lost all my trust Diane and there is no way I will ever trust you to tell me the truth ever again."

"Please Frank, there has to be some way to put us back together. I'll do anything Frank; anything at all."

"Sorry Diane, but there is no chance of our getting back together because I don't want to put us back together. The sight of you with your legs wrapped around North and the sound of your voice as you begged him to fuck you harder killed all the feelings I had for you. Look on the bright side. You are free to indulge in satisfying your curiosity whenever you want now. Just not here in this house. This house is neutral territory. You take your men elsewhere and I won't bring my women here."

"Your women?"

"I have no intention of going without a sex life. I'm not a bad looking guy and I've had chances up the kazoo to play around, but I never did because I promised during our wedding ceremony that I'd be faithful to you. You made the same vows, but you broke them. When you broke your vows you released me from mine. At least I won't be bringing mine in here where you can see it."

She looked at me and I could tell what she was thinking. She was thinking that sharing the house and being around each other would give her a chance to work her way back into my life and that is just what I wanted her to think. I decided to give her a load to carry.

"The only reason I'm doing this share the house thing is that I don't want to make the lawyers rich by going through a divorce and I don't want to give up what I have here at the house to live in an apartment. I wouldn't have a garage to work in, a basement workshop and I wouldn't have a patio where I can sit and enjoy a drink as I watch the sun set. You have two choices Diane; live with the new status quo or not. If you chose not then you can either move out or take over the house payments and expenses and I'll move out.

"You say that you really do love me so here is your chance to prove it. You can accept home sharing or you can take the house and cost me my garage, my workshop and my patio just like you cost me my wife. Your choice."

"There is no chance?"

"I don't see how there could be Diane."

She was silent for a few moments and then she opened her mouth and drove the final nail into her coffin.

"What are you going to do with the pictures Frank?"

"The pictures?"

"The ones you took with your cell phone camera."

She hadn't even talked to North since he ran out of the house? Then how did she know about the cell phone pictures? That was a story made up by Arlis and fed to her husband a good five days after I'd caught Diane and North in our bedroom. No indeed. I could not trust anything Diane told me ever again.

I could not physically hurt her and kicking her out of the house would cost me more than it would punish her, but being around me all the time while I ignored her would put her through a mental hell and that was the best I could hope for. I did not doubt that she loved me and I knew she would hang in there on the remote chance that she might eventually work her way back into my good graces. It wasn't going to happen. I was not kidding when I said that seeing her with North had killed all my feelings for her, but the longer she held on hoping the longer my revenge would last.

My revenge against Diane in place I turned my attention to Stanton North.

***

The private detective's report backed up what I had suspected. Getting caught by me and his wife finding out that he was a cheating asshole had not slowed him down a single bit. He was laying pipe to five women besides his wife. In the three weeks I'd had the PIs on him he hadn't done a thing with Diane, but he was nailing two of her co-workers. One of them, Mary Ellen Bingham had a husband that worked the afternoon shift and every Tuesday and Thursday after work North would pay Mary Ellen a visit at her home on Sunflower Way. He stayed two hours and then left.

I checked my watch and saw that if he kept to his schedule he would be out of the house in ten minutes. I was parked one block away and one block over. I got out of my car and made my way over to the Bingham residence went around behind the garage and when I got there I slipped on the latex gloves and put on a ski mask.

Mary Ellen had a three car garage and when North visited he pulled into the garage and parked and closed the garage door so the neighbors wouldn't get to talking about Mary Ellen's visitor. Wouldn't want the word to get back to Mary Ellen's hubby now would we? I used a small pry bar to force the lock on the back door to the garage and I was waiting when the connecting door to the house opened and North came out. A naked Mary Ellen stood in the doorway and watched North walk to his car.

Fifty thousand volts from the Taser had him writhing on the garage floor and before Mary Ellen could even scream I said in what I hoped was a disguised voice:

"Scream or call the cops and your hubby will find out what has been going on. Best you go back in the house and pretend that nothing is going on out here. I won't kill him, but you can be sure that another husband that he has stabbed in the back is getting even."

She jumped backwards and slammed the door. Mary Ellen knew me from all the company picnics and Christmas parties that Diane had taken me to, but I was counting on the ski mask and the disguised voice to keep her from knowing who was fucking over her fuck buddy. I couldn't count on her not calling the police so I had to hurry. I pulled North's pants off of him and believe me when I tell you that pulling pants off of a guy in convulsions isn't easy.

Once I had his pants off I took my revenge.

Proud of his package was he? Well his package was going to pay. I took the fully charged cattle prod and touched it to his cock and balls as many times as I could until it was fully discharged. I kicked him twice in the ribs for the hell of it and then I took his wallet and checkbook and got the hell out of there. I heard no sirens so maybe Mary Ellen didn't call the cops.

As I drove away I thought about what I had just done. I had no idea how much damage, if any, that the cattle prod would cause and whether or not there would be any lasting effects, but I can honestly say that I enjoyed every one of North's screams when a cattle prod charge flashed through his cock and balls.

I never did hear how Mary Ellen made out on the deal. Was she able to get North out of there and keep her husband in the dark or did she have to call for medical attention for North and have to explain an ambulance at the house to her hubby?

Still wearing the latex gloves I put the wallet and checkbook in a package I had already prepared and sent it to Arlis at her office. There was no note enclosed and I would deny I knew anything about it, but when her hubby came home hurting and then his wallet showed up in the mail she would think she knew who had done it.

***

Three weeks after my little party with North I got a phone call from Arlis.

"You busy for lunch?"

"I haven't made any plans; why?"

"I think it is time for us to have a face to face. How about noon at the Lido? I'll be the redhead anxiously checking out every man who walks in to see if I can figure out which one is you."

"Noon it is."

I didn't see her anxiously checking faces, but she was easy to spot since she was the only redhead in the place sitting alone. North was a flaming idiot to be screwing around on her. She was drop dead gorgeous. I walked up to her table.

"Mrs. North?"

"No Frank; it is Arlis. You haven't called me Mrs. North since our first phone conversation."

I took a seat across from her and said, "Might I ask what prompted you to ask me to lunch?"

"I just wanted a good look at the man who keeps screwing up my life."

"I'm screwing up your life? How am I doing that?"

"First you made me pull my head out of the sand and face up to what I was fairly sure he was doing, but hoped he wasn't. Then, after I let him talk me into giving him one more chance, you took away the best thing that he had going for him."

"I don't understand."

"Sure you do. Stan is a good provider and a pretty decent father to our kids, but the best thing that he had going for him was that he was great in bed. Notice that I said "was?""

"And I took it away? How did I do that?"

"Don't play the innocent with me Frank. We both know who did a number on Stan's private parts."

"I don't have a clue as to what you are talking about."

"Sure you don't. Anyway, ever since you did whatever it was that you did to him he has not been able to get it up and don't give me any of that crap about not knowing what I'm talking about. Wallets in the mail are kind of your trademark."

Just then the waitress walked up to take our order. As Arlis ordered a salad and ice tea I gave her a good once over. Yes indeed, her husband was an idiot not to have stayed home. As well as being gorgeous Arlis was pretty sharp as I quickly found out.

"Well?" she asked.

"Well what?"

"Do I pass?"

"What are you talking about now?"

"What? I wasn't supposed to notice you checking me out just now?"

I was caught and I knew it so I just gave her a goofy smile and said, "Who? Me?"

"Yes you and I hope you like what you see because the real reason for this little get together is to offer it to you."

I don't know what the look on my face was saying to her, but she went on:

"I am a very sexual person with a very high sex drive and since you have taken my play toy away from me I feel that it is only fair that you take over his duties."

That caught me flat-footed and I didn't know what to say. She smiled at me and said:

"I'll bet you weren't expecting that one were you?"

"To be honest, it never entered my mind."

"Well Frank, here is the way I see it. You deprived me of my bed partner so it is only fair that you take his place and second, what can be a more fitting way to get back at your wife and my husband?"

"I don't know Arlis. The package is outstanding, but I don't know that it is a good idea. The situation that I'm in right now could be upset if I give Diane grounds to sue for divorce."

"You aren't divorcing her?"

I explained what I was doing and she laughed. "You are evil aren't you, but not to worry. I don't intend to broadcast it. If Stan never gets the use of his equipment back I'll divorce him and I don't want him to have grounds to counter sue either."

"You are serious about this?"

"You betcha!"

And that is how my Affair with Arlis North started. It has been going on for over a year now and it doesn't show any sign of ending any time soon. Her husband still hasn't been able to get an erection. The doctors say there is no physical reason for him not to be able to perform so his problem is probably mental. Arlis says she will give him until the end of the year and then if he still can't get it up he will be history.

As far as I know Diane hasn't been seeing anyone, but she is well aware that I'm seeing someone, but she has no idea who. The knowledge that I am having sex with another woman is killing her, but she keeps hanging on hoping for a miracle that is never going to come.

I couldn't ask for better revenge.

End of the 5th Story

Anna's Overnight

I knew better. I'd watched friends and co-workers make the same mistake for years and I still went ahead and did it. And even though what had happened to them also happened to me, I didn't care. In fact, what had ended in divorce for most of them ended up making my marriage stronger.

I am an airline employee and have been one for over thirty years. And among the lower orders (that is everyone except pilots) it is a basic article of faith that you never, and I do mean never, take up with a stew. A stew (they prefer to be called flight attendants, but no one in the industry calls them anything but stews) will break your heart - it's a given. Marry a stew and your life becomes one of misery and frustration. Let me hastily add here that it is not always the stew's fault, a lot of the time it is the nature of a stew's job and what that job will cause when it comes up against human nature. The nature of a stew's job is travel, and in traveling she will sometimes be required to stay overnight at far away cities and some times, depending on her seniority, her trips can keep her away from home for days. These things don't matter in the first year or two of marriage, while the full bloom of love clouds your mind, but eventually the green eyed monster will rear its ugly head. She will become suspicious of what he is doing while she is gone, sometimes justified and sometimes not, or he will be the one to become suspicious of what she is doing, again sometimes justified and sometimes not. Anyway, I'd have to say that 85 to 90 percent of all the marriages that involve stews that I know of have ended in separation or divorce.

A case in point - my friend Jack. He and Mary were married in June of 1998. That they loved each other was clear to everyone who knew them, but in less than a year they were separated. Why? Because of time and distance. Mary would be gone three or four days at a time and when she would call home Jack wouldn't be there. Flight crews usually stay at a given hotel on RON's (remain over nights). These hotels are selected by airline management and are under contract to provide X many rooms every night for the flight crews. Jack would call the hotel and not be able to get in touch with Mary. Before long Mary got suspicious - she couldn't get ahold of Jack because he was out running around with other women. Jack got suspicious of Mary - he couldn't get in touch with her because she was shacked up with the pilot, copilot or a lover she had met and started an affair with. When Mary would get home from a trip, instead of a joyful reunion, the two of them fought, accused, and argued. Was Mary fucking around on her trips? Was Jack running around on her when she was gone? Who knows. Bottom line - don't get involved with a stew and that was a rule that I steadfastly adhered to - until I met Anna.

Our first encounter was not an auspicious one. My shift started at eleven p.m. and my assignment for the night was to perform a Service Check on an MD-80 that included several time changes including a CSD and a Fuel Control Unit. Even with help from a couple of other guys I didn't get it done until nearly five -thirty and the aircraft had to be on the gate by six. I cleaned up and we pushed the aircraft out of the hanger and I taxied it to the gate. As was my habit, I stuck a can of coffee in the coffee maker so the crew would have hot coffee when they came on board. I took a paperback out of my back pocket and settled down in the aisle seat of the first row in the first class section to wait for the crew. About ten minutes later I heard the stews coming up the airstairs and when they got to the galley area I saw that one of them was Ramona Winters and I cursed my luck. Ramona was an evil bitch who was sweet as sugar to the paying passengers, but downright nasty to everyone else, especially aircraft mechanics. She walked up to me and said, "Who the fuck told you that you could start the coffee maker?"

Having previously experienced Ramona's displeasure, and not having liked it one bit, I said, "Eat shit and die Winters. Till the captain or first officer get here this is my aircraft and I'll do what I damn well please."

She responded with, "You can't talk to me like that. I want you off this aircraft right now!"

"You sure?" I asked.

"Damn right!" she said.

I shrugged and got up from my seat and on my way to the cockpit I saw, for the first time, one of the other stews, one that I had never seen before. About 5'2", 110 pounds, soft brown hair and brown eyes, a very nice figure and a face that captured my heart. Not gorgeous, not really beautiful, but wholesome, cute, a real girl next door face. Under other circumstances I would have stopped and introduced myself, but not that morning. That morning I was going to stuff a poker up Ramona's ass. I went into the cockpit and shut down the APU. That killed all power except ground power to the aircraft and then I hit the switch that killed ground power.

"Hey! What are you doing?" hollered Ramona.

"Leaving the aircraft sweetie, just like you wanted."

"Put the power back on before you go."

I laughed, "Sorry Ramona. You are trained to give first aid, serve meals and drinks, and a whole bunch of other stuff, but you don't know how to handle an APU fire and a few other things that might happen with an APU running. Since the aircraft is my responsibility till the captain or first officer get here and you want me gone, the power stays off."

I got off the plane and went into the gate area where I read my book until the FO got there.

"Why is the power off?" he wanted to know.

"Ramona doesn't want me on the plane so since I can't monitor APU operation from here I shut it down."

He muttered, "Fucking bitch" as he went up the airstair.

Two days later I was having breakfast in the airport employee's cafeteria when one of the other guys said, "Don't look now, but I think you have an admirer. She hasn't taken her eyes off you since she sat down."

I looked and it was the cute, wholesome looking girl who had been present during the Ramona incident. I got up and asked her to join us, one thing led to another and six months later we were married. From the beginning I could tell that our marriage wasn't going to be like any of the others where a stew was involved. I was always at home when she called, and she called every night she was gone. I rarely called her, but when I did she was always there. When she got home we were so damn glad to see each other that we sometimes forgot that there were other people in the world. In bed and out, we could not get enough of each other. At the end of four years of marriage we still could not keep our hands off each other. By the end of that fourth year Anna was off reserve status and had enough seniority to bid for a block of her own. Unfortunately, that block that she was flying was going to have her out of town on our fifth wedding anniversary. She tried to work a trade, but couldn't, so we planned on celebrating when she got home.

The day she left on her trip I was finally able to work a day trade with another mechanic and I caught a flight for SFO which is where she was going to overnight. When I got to the hotel where the crews were being put up I looked into the restaurant and saw Anna eating dinner with the rest of the crew and I started to go in and join them, but then I had a better idea. I went to the desk and identified myself and said that my wife was supposed to have left me a key. The desk clerk made me show him my I.D. and then he gave me a key and I hurried up to the room. There is no place to hide in a hotel room so I figured I lie down on the floor on the far side of the bed and when Anna came in I'd jump up and yell "Happy Anniversary." It was almost half an hour before I heard a key in the lock and I got down on the floor and got ready. The door opened and I heard, "Hurry up! I want your cock in me. I need to be fucked."

"Oh shit!" I thought, I'm in the wrong room.

A male voice said, "Damn it, at least let me get my pants off."

"Well hurry up and get them off while I call my husband."

It was Anna's voice.   There were sounds of undressing, the phone being dialed, and a long pause and then Anna said, "He's not answering. That's strange, he's always there."

The man said, "Maybe he's out getting some strange pussy, maybe he's trying to stay even with you."

Anna laughed, "Not my hubby.   When I'm home I fuck him to death.   I don't leave him with enough strength to go after anyone else. Now get over here and fuck me."

For the next five minutes I laid there and listened to the sounds of flesh smacking flesh and Anna moaning "Oh yes, oh yes, oh yes" and finally I couldn't take it anymore.   I raised my head just enough to see over the edge of the bed and I saw a naked Anna being fucked by a middle aged man that I recognized as a captain for our airline. Anna had her legs locked behind his and her hands were on his shoulders. Her face was in my direction, but her eyes were closed and I watched for a moment more.   Just as I was about to duck my head back down her eyes opened and our gazes locked.   There was no change in her facial expression, but with her eyes locked on mine, seeming to stare in at my very soul, she cried, "Fuck me baby, fuck me hard. Give me your cock. Harder baby, harder. Make your little slut cum."

Her eyes never left mine and I couldn't tear mine away from hers. Her partner was pounding hard now and Anna cried, "Fill me up baby, fill me up.   Give me your cum lover, cum in me baby" and apparently he did for she switched to, "Oh yes, oh yes, that's so good. You feel so good inside me." Her eyes broke from mine and I sank back to the floor and became aware, for the first time, that my cock was rock hard. I lay there listening to their small talk:

He: "God! What got into you? You've never been that wild or vocal before."

Anna: "It was your beautiful cock lover. It touched something it never touched before,"

He: "Well I hope it happens again, it was great!"

Anna: "It will baby. You know you can fuck me anytime you want. I hate to rush you baby, but I've still got to try and reach my hubby. After all, it is our anniversary."

He: "How about tomorrow? We don't fly until ten fifteen."

Anna: "Sure baby. I left a seven o'clock wake up call. Just knock twice and my pussy is all yours."

I heard the door open and then close and then Anna rolled over and looked down at me, "Don't say anything. Just get up here and fuck me."

I started to say something but she said, "No! Not now. Just get your cock out and fuck me. Come on baby, get up here and fuck the slut that you married."

I should have been upset and angry over her betrayal, but I didn't think of that as I climbed up on the bed. All I could think of was putting my cock into the unfaithful bitch. I didn't even take off my clothes; I just pulled down my zipper and moved between her spread legs. There was no resistance as my cock slid into her wet box and as soon as I was in she locked her legs behind mine and her hands grabbed my ass.

"Oh yes, oh yes, oh god baby, fuck your whorish wife. Oh yes baby, harder, that's it, fuck me harder. Do you feel him baby, can you feel his cum? You like sloppy seconds baby? Oh god yesssss" and she had an orgasm - her body shook so hard that she almost threw me off of her. "Oh god baby, don't stop, don't stop, keep fucking your little slut, fuck me, fuck me, fuck me."

She had another orgasm and then I came into her as hard as I had ever cum before in my life, but I didn't go soft. "Don't stop baby, don't stop, please don't stop. I need you in me, come on baby, fuck me, fuck your whore."

It took me another twenty minutes before I came for the second time and still my dick stayed hard as Anna kept begging for more and more fucking and for me to fuck her harder and faster.

"Oh god baby, yes, yes, yes, you feel so good in me. You like fucking me after somebody else, don't you? You like soaking your cock in another man's cum. Come on baby, fuck me."

It was a long night and I finally collapsed, drained and exhausted. Anna still wanted more and she started sucking my cock and it was beginning to show signs of life when I fell asleep.

The phone woke me up and I looked at the bedside clock; it was seven a.m. Anna, who had been curled up against me, the same as she did at home, rolled over and grabbed the phone, "Thank you operator" she said and hung up the phone. She looked over at me and we stared at each other for several moments and then her hand went to my cock, which went instantly erect. She began to stroke it as she said, "I'm sorry that you had to find out about me baby. I never wanted you to know what a slut I am." She moved over me and lowered herself onto my hardness as she continued, "I know you probably hate me now and I can't - "Oh yes, like that, just like that" as I thrust myself up into her, "Oh yes baby, oh god honey, don't stop, please don't stop. Fuck me baby, fuck me" and she started riding my cock.

We had been at it for two or three minutes when there was a knock at the door - two quick taps. Anna pulled herself off me, "Quick baby, on the floor."

I looked at her in confusion and she pushed me to the edge of the bed, "On the floor, hurry!" and I rolled off onto the floor. A few seconds later my clothes landed on top of me and I heard the door open.

"Jesus, it's about time you got here. I'm so horny that I almost called room service so I could fuck the waiter."

He said, "God, but you are wet." Anna replied, "Honey, I've been laying here all night wanting your cock. I wished I'd have let you stay. It would have been a kick to have your cock buried in me while my hubby was wishing me a happy anniversary. Maybe we could do it tonight. Would you like that? Would you like to slide your cock into me while I talk to my hubby on the phone?"

He laughed, "God, but you are such a slut."

Anna giggled, "I know baby, but that's why you like me, isn't it? Come on baby, fuck me."

Trusting that she would turn so he wouldn't be looking my way while he dicked her, I looked over the edge of the bed and watched the two of them go at it. I was just as turned on as I had been the night before and I did not understand any of it. The lying, cheating whore had been fucking around on me and I should have been angry enough to stand up and kick both of their asses, but instead I laid there next to the bed wishing the asshole would hurry up and get his rocks off so I could slide into Anna's cum filled pussy again.

"Fuck me baby, fuck me hard. Think about tonight. I'll be leaning on my elbows and you'll be fucking me in my asshole while I talk to my hubby on the phone. Yes, yes, that's it baby, cum for me, cum for me, fill me with your hot cum."

Finally he shot his load and I sank back down onto the floor and listened to the kiss and make small talk. She finally told him he had to leave so she could get ready and he left.

"Hurry honey, get up here and fuck me" and I did. It lasted almost half an hour before I came and then Anna jumped up and headed for the shower. I started to say something, but she cut me off, "Not now honey, not now. I'll call you from Kansas City tonight, but I have to run" and then she was in the bathroom and the door closed behind her.

The flight home and then the long wait for Anna's phone call were agonizing. What was I going to say? What was she going to say? I remembered her saying that she had never wanted me to find out what a slut she was; how long had this been going on? Was her marriage to me and all the happiness we had shared just a sham? Jesus, I couldn't bear it if that were true. I loved her more that I had ever loved anyone else or anything in my life. I thought about my many years of saying, "Stay away from stews, they'll only break your heart" and I kicked myself for not taking my own advice. The only thing I knew for sure was that when she called me she was going to have a cock buried in her ass and the idea of that both pissed me off and excited the hell out of me. I was never more than two feet from the phone all day and when the call did come I snatched the cordless like a drowning man grabbing a life preserver. "Hello?"

"Hi baby. Do you miss me? Do you wish I were there so I could suck your cock? Don't you wish you could suck my pussy and fuck me in my ass? You like my ass don't you baby? I've got something in my ass right now and it feels so good. It's a big dildo that I got to remind me of you."

I could hear little grunts and quivers in her voice and knew she was being fucked and without even realizing it I had my cock out and was stroking it.

"You still there baby? You miss me, you want me?"

In a voice so hoarse that I didn't recognize it I croaked, "You fucking slut. I hope you are enjoying that cock in your ass. When you get home I'm going to fuck it so much that no one else will ever be able to touch the sides."

"Oh baby, you say the sweetest things. I'll see you tomorrow and my ass will be hot, wet, and waiting. I love you, bye." And as the phone clicked I shot cum out of the head of my dick so hard that I'm surprised that it didn't hit the ceiling.

She walked in the door a little past noon and her flight bag hadn't hit the floor and she was peeling off her uniform. Her eyes looking into mine she said, "You want my ass baby? You want to put your cock in my ass and feel what John left in there for you? He fucked me twice this morning and both loads are still there. I haven't gone to the bathroom because I wanted to save him for you. I want you to feel John's cum in me baby, I want you to feel his cum around your cock. Come on baby, come and fuck the whore that you married."

By the time she finished talking she was naked and had dropped to the floor, head cradled on her hands and her ass stuck up in the air. "Come on baby, your unfaithful little slut wants you in her ass. Come on baby, fuck my well used ass."

I fell on her with a fury. I made no attempt to be gentle or ease my way in as I usually did; I just rammed myself into her as hard as I could. She gave a little cry of pain and it very quickly turned into a low moan and then she was talking again, "Oh god yes baby, that feels so good. Fuck my slutty ass baby, fuck me. Feel John's cum baby. He fucked my ass real good last night. He was laughing while I talked to you and he was fucking me. Did you like that baby? Did you like talking to me while another man was fucking me in my ass?"

I was in frenzy now; I was fucking the unfaithful bitch as hard as I could. I wanted her to cry out, "Easy baby, you're hurting me," but she didn't. The harder I fucked her the more she cried, "oh god yes, oh yes, oh yes, don't stop baby, don't stop, fuck my ass, fuck my ass." She had already cum three times and I still hadn't cum.

"Oh baby," she said, "You must like knowing that I've been fucked by someone else. I do it a lot baby. Do you like knowing that?

That I get fucked by someone else on every trip? Aah, that's good baby, fuck me baby, fuck me."

The knowledge that she had been fucking around on me all along drove me over the edge and I came so hard that it actuality hurt. I collapsed on the living room floor and Anna got up and went into the bathroom.

I was still lying on the floor, breathing hard, when she came back with a wash rag and cleaned off my cock. She knelt down and started sucking me and when she eventually got it hard she straddled me and sat on it. She just sat there looking at me and then she said, "Have I lost you?"

I was quiet for a moment and then I said, "Why do you care? By last count we had over six hundred pilots and copilots, that ought to be enough to keep you happy."

A hurt look showed on her face and she said, "I don't love any of them baby. I love you and you are the only man I've ever loved. I never wanted you to find out about my other side. I've tried hard to be a good wife to you and to keep you happy, but I'm a cock hungry slut. I can't get enough cock. I don't give a shit about any of the rest of those guys I see, they are just dicks to me, pieces of meat to satisfy my craving to be fucked. I don't want to lose you baby, honest to God I don't. I love you so much that sometimes it hurts."

I was quiet as I looked up at the woman I loved more than life itself - the woman who had, by her own admission, been fucking around on me all these years. What could I say that would mean anything? Lamely I said, "When did it start? When did you start fucking around on me?"

"The day we met lover. In college I was the sweetheart of half the fraternities on campus - you needed to get laid? Go see Anna, she'll help you out. Take some friends with you because she loves to fuck. When I graduated I knew I had to change my life style or I'd end up a diseased old hag so I applied for a job as a flight attendant. I figured the pilots would be married so there would be no romantic entanglements and they have yearly physicals so they would likely be disease free. If a pilot had a disease and got found out the airline would get rid of him. Hell, all of management flew before becoming management, they know what goes on out there and the last thing they would want is for disease to be passed among the crews. My very first trip the captain fucked me and I've been fucked on every trip since then. Captains, first officers, flight engineers and even some of the male flight attendants. On some occasions it was more than one of them at the same time. I love cock baby. I can't get enough!"

"I can't believe this."

"It's true baby, I wish it wasn't, but it's true. I fell for you the morning that you told Ramona to eat shit and when you asked me to marry you it was the happiest day of my life. I couldn't tell you what I was - you would have run from me screaming and I'd never have seen you again. I thought I could hide that part of me from you. It only happened out of town and the flight crews don't socialize with the mechanics and rampys so I knew you would never hear the gossip about me. When I saw you in that hotel room I died inside; I knew that I'd lost you, but then I thought that if I acted as slutty as I could you might just be fascinated enough to stick around long enough for me to do something so I could hang on to you." She stopped riding up and down on my cock and looked at me, "You're not listening to me, are you? You're gone - I've lost you."

Tears started rolling down her cheeks and she sobbed and tried to stand up. I grabbed her and pulled her back and hugged her to my chest.

I'm watching Monday Night Football and both teams suck. I looked at my watch and only a minute has passed since I last looked five minutes ago. The phone rings and I grabbed the cordless "Hello?"

"Hi baby. Thinking of me? Thinking about how you would like

to be sliding you cock into my pussy? I'm so hot thinking about you and my pussy is so wet it feels like I have three loads of cum in me. Are you thinking of me baby?"

"God Anna," I croak out, "You are such a fucking slut."

"I know baby, but that's why you love me, isn't it?"

End of the 6th Story

What I Came Home To

It had been a bad day all around. The car had a dead battery when I left the house to go to work. I got a ration of shit from my foreman for being late to work and thirty minutes before quitting time I cut my arm so bad that I had to have four stitches. I got home to find my wife not there and my dinner not ready which I admit is no big thing in the great scheme of life, but it was my bowling night and for the last six years the pattern was I came home to a ready dinner, grabbed my bowling shirt and split for the bowling alley getting there just in time for the start of the early league. Ten minutes after I got home Shelly came in with an arm full of packages from the stores at the mall. Normally I am a calm, quiet guy and I tend to think before I speak, but it had been a bad day and dinner not waiting and Shelly shopping was just too much.

"Damn it Shelly, I told you that we needed to watch the budget. What the hell are you doing out spending money instead of being here fixing dinner. You know it is my bowling night."

It was stupid of me and I knew it before the words were completely out of my mouth. Shelly's response was as predictable as was my response to her response. Voices got louder and the conversation, if it could be called that, got more and more heated. By the time I grabbed my bowling ball and slammed the front door behind me the temperature in the house was below freezing.

The drive to the bowling alley gave me time to realize that I had let the happenings of the day put me in a foul mood and I'd let that foul mood rob me of my common sense. I'd had no good reason to jump Shelly the way I had and over something stupid like my dinner not being ready at that. Now I was going to have to crawl on my knees to try and fix my fuck up.

The God's must have decided that I needed some cheering up

and so they smiled down on me. I carry a 173 average and rarely does a week go by that I don't have a game in the high 190s or low 200s, but that night I found my groove. My first game was a 256 and I followed it with a 237 in the second game, but it was the third game that made my night. The tension mounted as I threw strike after strike after strike. I had seven in a row and my palms were sweaty as I contemplated my first ever 300 game. In the eighth frame I knew as soon as I released the ball that I was fucked. I had hit one board to the left of my spot and as I stood there and watched I thought oh well, maybe next time. But the God's were still smiling down on me. The ball came in on the Brooklyn side of the head pin, I got good pin action and all of those puppies went down. I began to think I could do no wrong. The ninth frame was another strike off of a poorly thrown ball and I just knew it was my destiny to roll that 300. Bowling out in the tenth I threw two more strikes and suddenly the sweaty palms were back and no amount of playing with the rosin bag would dry them. I eyed my spot, looked down the alley, took a deep breath and went. The approach was perfect, the release a thing of beauty and then I stood there and watched as the ball made its way down the alley. It was absolutely and without a doubt the most perfect ball I had ever rolled. It tracked down my grove, came straight in at the pocket and then the crack of the hit and pins flying everywhere and when all the action was done I stood there and stared. The fucking ten pin was still standing. The most perfect ball I'd ever thrown and it left a fucking ten pin. For an instant I was one highly pissed individual and then I remembered that Brooklyn hit from the eighth and shrugged. It all evens out. Besides, a 792 series isn't anything to sneeze at and as a consolation I took all four jackpots that night. The team retired to the bar and we celebrated for a couple of hours.

I was in a great mood on the drive home and I knew just what to do to start working my way back into Shelly's good graces. She was usually asleep when I got home, but that night I was going to wake her up. I would do it by doing what Shelly loved the most – I would eat her pussy. The house was dark when I got there. I put my bowling ball in the hall closet and quietly entered the dark bedroom. I heard Shelly's even breathing and it indicated that she was sound asleep. I undressed and pulled the sheet off her and then slowly worked her underpants down. She must have been really pissed at me; she always sleeps naked and never wears panties to bed unless she plans on denying me sex. I grinned, let's see her try to deny me when she wakes up with my tongue in her box.

I eased her legs apart and moved in to position. Her pussy smelled a little different that night and I couldn't quite place my finger on why I thought that. She was wet, very wet, when my tongue probed the folds of her pussy and she moaned and her pussy seemed to rise up to meet me. I wanted to be firmly in control when she woke up so I slid my hands under her ass and pulled her to me and then I got busy eating pussy. I heard a couple of grunts, a snort and then, "Wha…, oh, oh, oh" and hands grabbed my head and held me in place. At that exact instant that the hands grabbed my head I realized why her cunt smelled different and why she was so wet. I had just tasted the wetness and I knew what it was! She had been very recently fucked and I was licking up another man's cum!

It is hard to try and explain the thoughts that roar through your head at a time like that. The emotion is anger and rage, but the thoughts are a jumbled mess and they all run together. In no particular order they were:

-The bitch had been so mad at me that she had gone out and let another man fuck her. Then she had come home and gone to bed with her panties on to tell me that I wasn't going to be getting any pussy for a while.

-Had she done this before? I'd never know because the "no panties, no sex" was a given after we'd had an argument.

-Did she get mad and just go out and get laid, or did she have a regular lover?

-She hadn't showered when she got home. Was she getting some perverse kick out of lying next to me in bed with another man's cum soaking her insides?

-Did I really know what she did on the nights that I bowled?

-She had cum in her. Did she have unprotected sex every time she fucked another guy? Was that another kick of hers – to let me possibly raise some other guy's kid?

-Just how fresh was the stuff? How long had she been home, or had she even gone out? Had she fucked him here in our own bed?

Was it a white man's cum? She'd told me once about s fling she'd had in college with a black basketball player. Was there any truth to the "once you go black you'll always go back?"

All of that shit bounced around in my head in the time it took Shelly to go from, "Wha…" to "oh, oh, oh." The natural reaction probably would have been for me to leap out of the bed, turn on the light and scream, "You fucking whore! Who was it?"

But I had a hard on and I was ready to fuck and since this might be my last time until after the divorce and I could find someone else I decided to make the best of it. Don't get me wrong here, I didn't have a hard cock over the fact that I was sucking up another man's leavings; my cock had been hard since I started home from the bowling alley thinking about how I was going to make up with Shelly. Besides, I'd never had sloppy seconds before, at least not that I knew of, and I was just a little curious.

I redoubled my efforts on Shelly's unfaithful cunt. Give her something to remember me by. She was writhing and humping her pussy at my mouth as I licked and sucked away at her. Her grunts and "oh, ohs" were all I was getting out of her which was strange because Shelly was usually very vocal. Was she feeling guilty knowing that I was sucking up her lover's sauce?

My cock was throbbing and I was ready to fuck, but I always made sure that I got Shelly off when I ate her and not to do it this time might have made her suspicious and I didn't want that. I was going to leave her unfaithful ass, but not until I had all my ducks in a row. I latched onto her clit and sucked hard at it while shoving a finger up Shelly's ass and she screamed and had her orgasm. She wasn't down from her high yet when I climbed on and shoved my cock into her. It slid right in her already well lube hole and I held myself still for a second or two to feel the sensation of another man's cum around my cock and then I began to fuck her.

I slammed into the bitch as hard as I could and with each stroke she emitted a loud grunt and then her legs locked around me, her nails bit into my ass and she screamed out, "Oh God yes, oh sweet fucking Jesus yes!" as she had another orgasm. It didn't register on me until my cum was already boiling up out of my balls that Shelly had screamed out those words. Shelly had always been loudly vocal during the act, but only noises, never words. Was the cunt so turned on by the fact she was fucking me with her lover's cum still inside her that she was changing her personality?

I drained into her and then went to get up, but she grabbed me and pulled me back down. The whore wanted me to eat her again. Well, what the fuck, it wasn't going to happen again very often since I figured to be moved out in less than a week so down I went. I licked and slurped and sucked as Shelly pushed her cunt up at me and dug her fingers in my hair and clutched me to her. I attacked her pussy. I'd give her an orgasm that she would never forget – one she could think of on the nights that I'd no longer be around. She had once told me that she could never get any of her boyfriends to go down on her and that for her to have found me and that I loved to do it was a gift from the gods. With any kind of luck (from my point of view) she would never find anyone else who would do it for her, let alone do it and love doing it. The fucking slut could play with herself and suffer as she remembered what she'd had in me. My jaw was getting sore and I knew it was time for me to stop and I sent my finger on its way to Shelly's asshole, but before it could get there she had another orgasm. I waited until her breathing steadied and then I started to raise myself up and she said, "Sweet fucking Jesus. I've never felt anything like that before in my life."

I was on my knees looking down on the dark form lying on the bed. My mind was in turmoil and I didn't know what to do. The voice wasn't Shelly's! The woman in my bed wasn't my wife.

I stumbled off the bed and turned on the light. Lying on the bed and looking at me with a bemused smile on her face was Marlene, my best friend's wife.

"No wonder Shelly is always walking around with a big smile on her face. That was something baby; that was mind blowing."

"What are you doing here? Why are you in our bed?"

"Strictly an accident lover. A happy accident, at least for me, but an accident none the less. I must have gotten mixed up when I went to the bathroom and ended up in the wrong bed."

"But why are you here?"

"Shelly's mom had an accident and Shelly had to pick her up and take her to the hospital emergency room. She tried reaching you at the bowling alley, but for some reason couldn't. She called Doug to see if he would run over and let you know, but he had the carb off his truck and he needed to get it fixed for work tomorrow so I volunteered to come over here and wait for you to get home. I got sleepy and I lay down on the bed in the spare bedroom. I got up to go to the bathroom and must have gotten turned around and so here we are. Could you tell that Doug and I made love just before I came over here?"

I nodded a yes.

"The first time? You knew then?"

Again I nodded a yes.

"Doug has never eaten my pussy. I don't know what turned me on the most, getting my pussy eaten or knowing that you were eating me while I was full of Doug's sperm. It was wild lover and I've never felt like that before in my life. We have to do it again."

"Don't be silly Marlene, you are my best friend's wife."

"You have already fucked your best friend's wife and done a marvelous job of it I might add, and you have also eaten her to two tremendous orgasms so it shouldn't be a problem to do it again."

"It was an accident Marlene, it never should have happened."

"But it did happen lover and I want it to happen again."

"No Marlene, no way."

"Yes lover, way, and you know why? Because if you don't I'll tell Doug and Shelly that you came home all liquored up and raped me. I'll call the cops and tell them the same thing. They will haul you off and then take me to the hospital and get a culture from my vagina and guess whose DNA they will find? Look on the bright side lover, Doug tells me that I'm the hottest piece of ass he's ever found and you can have all of it you can handle. So, until I can find some way to get Doug to eat my pussy you get to do the honors. It won't be one way lover. To return the favor I'll fuck you blind. Now come on over here lover and make me scream again."

I shook my head no and was backing away from the bed when the phone rang. I picked up the bedside phone and found that it was Shelly calling from the hospital. I was talking to Shelly and not paying any attention to Marlene so it came as a complete surprise when I felt her mouth close around my cock. I tried to pull away, but Marlene had a death grip on my ass with both of her hands and she wasn't letting me go anywhere. There was a slight pause in the conversation on my end as I struggled to get away from Marlene and Shelly said, "What's wrong?"

"Nothing baby, I almost dropped the phone."

"Did Marlene tell you what is going on?"

"Yes. How is your mother?"

"She fell and hit her head. She is suffering from a mild

concussion and they don't want to release her for a bit. I'll be here at least two or three more hours. I'll see you in the morning. I love you, bye baby."

By the time I put the phone down Marlene had my cock as hard as a bar of iron and all of my blood was in the head of my dick and there was none left in the big head to keep my brain on the right track. I pushed Marlene back on the bed and mounted her and as my cock slid into her cunt I said, "You want it. You got it. Shelly won't be home for at least two hours so I'm going to do my best to send you home bow-legged."

"Just one more time lover and then I have to be going."

"Bullshit Marlene. You want to blackmail me for sex; sex is what you are going to get. What you tell Doug when you get home is your problem, but you aren't leaving this bed for another two hours."

She giggled, "Not even to go home and get another load from Doug so you can suck it out of me?"

"Tomorrow," I snarled as I began to pound into her cunt, "We can do that tomorrow."

End of the 7th Story

Beverly Gets a Surprise

I was just carrying the last of my things into Sarah's bedroom when I heard the garage door opener start to run. I glanced at my watch and saw that it was only ten-thirty and I thought "That sure didn't take long. Only three and a half hours to wreck a marriage that had lasted twenty-three years. Actually, it took less than five minutes.

I heard the door from the garage into the utility room open and then close and then I heard her high heels clicking across the tiled kitchen floor and then across the hardwood floor to the stairs. The heels made no noise on the carpeted steps, but I could still hear her coming.

As she made her way to what used to be our bedroom she had to pass the open door to Sarah's room and she noticed the light on and stopped to look in. She saw me putting my socks in the top drawer of the dresser and said:

"What are you doing Rob?"

"Putting my stuff away."

"Putting your stuff away? Why are you putting your stuff in Sarah's dresser?"

"It's my dresser now Beverly. This is my room now. At least it is until I can figure out what I want to do and where I want to move to."

"Move to? Have you lost your mind Rob?"

"No Beverly; that is what you did about four hours ago."

I thought back to almost four hours ago when I'd come home from work to find my Bev in her 'little black dress' and her sexiest high heels. I took in her get up and asked:

"What's up? I don't remember anything about us going somewhere. What did I forget?"

"You didn't forget anything. I'm going out. Your dinner is in the microwave. Just punch in three minutes."

"You are going out? Dressed like that?"

"What's wrong with the way I'm dressed?"

"That's how you dress when you expect that we will end up in bed making whoopee."

"I just wanted to look nice."

"Where are you going that you want to look that nice?"

"I'm just going to have dinner with a friend."

"What friend?"

"You don't know him."

"Him? Him? What the hell is going on here Bev? Why are you going out to dinner with a 'him' looking like that?"

"I didn't dress sexy. I just wanted to look nice."

"Look nice for him? What the fuck is going on here Beverly?"

"It's nothing Rob. One of the guys in the office asked me to have dinner with him and he is a nice guy so I thought it might be fun."

"Let me get this straight. A man you work with – a man who presumably knows that you are married – asked you to go out with him and you said yes? And you put on one of your sexiest outfits to wear when you go out with him?"

"Oh for God's sake Rob; its only dinner and maybe a few drinks."

"No Beverly; it isn't just dinner. It is a date with another man. A date with a man who knows that you are married. A date with a man who is thinking that a married woman willing to date is going to be an easy conquest and you dressing sexy is going to make him think that he is right."

"Damn it Rob; you are making this sound like I'm planning on cheating on you."

"Why wouldn't I think that? The way you are dressed for your date leads me to believe that you are considering doing just that. The fact that you are going out with another man leads me to believe that."

"Are you saying that you don't trust me?"

"I guess that is just what I'm saying."

"I have never given you a reason not to trust me."

"You are a grown woman Beverly and I don't own you. I cannot tell you what you can and can't do, but I can say that I am absolutely against it and if you do it there will be consequences."

"Get a grip Rob; it is just dinner with a friend."

"I've said my piece Beverly. It is up to you now."

I walked away from her and went into the den and put my briefcase on my desk. I hung my suit coat on the clothes tree and was on my way back to the kitchen when I heard the garage door start to operate. I shrugged, looked into the microwave and decided that what was in didn't look all that appetizing. I grabbed my car keys and headed out.

I had dinner at a Burger King and then I hit Home Depot on my way home and bought a lock set. When I got home I had to decide which room I wanted to move into. Billy was in the Navy and wouldn't be coming home until the cruise he was on was over and he could come home on leave. Sarah was married and would only be using her room when she and her husband came to visit and that only happened once or twice a year and always after plenty of notice so Sarah's room was my choice. By eight I had the lock set installed and had started moving my stuff.

Bev stood there watching me as I put the last of my socks in the drawer and then closed it.

"You are being stupid Rob. You are acting like a baby over nothing."

I was more than a little pissed with her so I decided to screw with her. I lied and said:

"Nothing? That's not the way I heard it. At least one person we know saw you with your date and called me. She said she was sorry to hear that we had broken up and I told her we hadn't and then asked her why she thought that we had. She said she saw you with another man holding hands and looking all dreamy eyed."

Bev didn't react with "That's a damned lie" so I went on:

"You should have at least touched up your lipstick before coming home and letting me see you. Now if you don't mind it is late and I need to get to bed."

I closed the door in her face, tripped the lock and went to bed.

***

I couldn't believe that he closed the door in my face. That was so not Rob. The man did not have a rude bone in his body so why had he done it? I may have badly misjudged things.

My Rob was not acting at all the way he was supposed to. He never fought me over what I did or wanted to do. That was one of the reasons I selected him to be my husband. God knows that I had plenty of other applicants for the position and quite frankly many of them were much better equipped than Rob, but I could tell that I wouldn't be able to control them after we got married.

Rob, while not overly well endowed, had enough to do an adequate job in the bedroom and he did have an added plus in that he did seem to really like eating my pussy. Another benefit was that he didn't get all bent out of shape when I wouldn't let him cum in my mouth. I swallowed for most of the rest of the guys I let bed me, but that was mostly because they were insistent on it and if they had any size to them I gave in so they would come back. I didn't dislike the taste of cum – in fact I really liked the taste – but it was a matter of control, By being able to refuse I was left with the feeling of being in charge and that was important to me.

The same thing went for my ass. Most of my lovers liked my ass and I enjoyed them playing there, but Rob never pushed when I told him no and I like that about him. It told me that I could be the one in charge and that Rob would go along with it.

I wasn't surprised when Rob asked me to marry him and I had pretty much already decided to lead him into doing just that when he did it on his own. I didn't say yes right away – the control thing again – and I planned on making him sweat a little before giving him the good news, but then Billy Neubert and Harry Short fucked that up for me. I was upstairs in a bedroom at a frat house with them and Billy was deep in my pussy while Harry was banging my ass when Harry said (as if I weren't even there):

"We need another cock for her so we can make her airtight" and Billy said (again – as if I weren't even there) "Let's get a bunch of guys together and gangbang her tomorrow."

"Hell of an idea. Who can we get?"

I know Sam wants a piece of her and I'll bet Frank, Joe, Larry and Stan would want in on it."

"Go ahead and set it up."

I should have protested, but they wouldn't have listened. Between them they had twenty-one inches of cock that they know I couldn't say no to so they were sure that I would go along with whatever they wanted. At that particular moment, given all the orgasms I was having, I probably would have agreed except for one thing. Rob!

Word seemed to get around about girls who pulled trains in frat houses and the last thing I needed was for Rob to find out about me and the extra boyfriends that he knew nothing about. I had to keep Billy and Harry from going out and asking a bunch of guys to gang fuck me. It also convinced me that I'd better lock Rob in sooner rather than later.

Three hours later when neither Harry nor Billy could answer the call any more I thanked them for a marvelous evening (and Oh God was it!) and then told them I wouldn't be seeing them anymore. They did not take it well, but so what! I called Rob as soon as I left the frat house and told him that yes, I would marry him.

After accepting Rob's proposal I was a good girl. Well, as good as I was capable of being. I only did a half a dozen guys, but I was very selective and only did the deed with the ones I knew would keep their mouths shut. I mean I was single and a girl needs to have her fun before she settles down right? However I doubted that Rob would see it that way.

I fully expected that the stripper at my bachelorette party was the last guy, except for Rob, that I would ever screw because I really did plan to honor my vows once I said "I do" and became Rob's wife. However, being the girl I was I did backslide a few times, but by and large I was a good girl. They were mostly one night stands when Rob was out of town on business although one was a pretty hot affair that lasted almost a year and I was pretty sure that Sarah was the product of it. Not that I ever let Gary know about it of course.

Just remembering Gary made my pussy tingle. A guy with eleven inches can do that to a girl. It happened at Rob's company Christmas party. Rob didn't pay much attention to his drinking and managed to get himself blotto and pass out. I'd had a few more than I should have and it made me loose and I was having fun dancing with Rob's co-workers and even let a few of them get a good feel of me when they got me under the mistletoe and kissed me. Gary, Rob's boss, was one of them. He managed to get me under the mistletoe three times and the third time he slipped me some tongue and I gave him some back.

By the end of the party I was hot enough to pull the train I'd never pulled at the frat house, but by then Rob was out of it so I was resigned to going home with the female version of blue balls. Gary volunteered to help me get Rob out to the car and after we had laid Rob on the back seat Gary pulled me into his arms and we kissed. We kissed passionately for several minutes before Gary said:

"It is a crying shame that a hot sexy woman like you has to go home from a fun party with no chance of finishing the night properly."

"Properly?"

"This is a night when you should have hot passionate love made to you. Obviously Rob won't be able."

"You're right. I guess I'll just have to go without."

"Not necessarily."

"What does that mean?"

"I'd be willing to volunteer."

I had been drinking, but not enough to cheat on Rob, especially with his boss, so I laughingly said:

"Sorry, but I only cheat on Rob with guys who have ten inches or better."

I expected him to say something like "I guess that leaves me out" or maybe "Damn it! Just my bad luck!" but instead he unzipped and pulled out his cock. Soft it was huge. "Will this do?" he asked as I watched it grow.

"You said at least ten and I have eleven when it is hard."

I was still watching it grow when he pushed me back on the front seat and pulled my panties off me. He did me right there on the front seat while Rob was passed out on the back. I came twice before he did and when he was done he pulled me up and said:

"I've got to have me some more of this. Rob will be okay where he is" and he took me by the hand and led me back into the hotel where the party had been held, got a room and fucked me three more times before I left and drove Rob home.

For the next year Gary sent Rob out of town frequently. There were others he could have sent, but he needed Rob gone so he could fuck me. I don't know how long it would have gone on if he hadn't been promoted and moved to corporate headquarters in Los Angeles. I was three months pregnant at the time, but wasn't showing so I never got to have the "Is it mine?" conversation with him.

I liked Rob a lot when I married him. It wasn't love, just a very strong like and again the only reason I married him was because I could control him. I quickly learned that I'd made the right choice. I could get whatever I wanted from Rob. He always gave in to me.

Over time the 'strong like' turned into love and we were happy together. True, I was a bit of a slut when he was out of town, but that didn't have any effect on the love I had for him. What I did on the side was for fun, not love.

As I climbed into bed I wondered if there was maybe some other way I should have gone about having my evening with Sean. I was so used to Rob giving in to me that I acted without thinking things through. What was really stupid about it was that nothing happened. Nothing was going to happen. At least not that night. It was an exploratory type thing to see if maybe I wanted to play with him.

Sheila from Accounting was telling the girls what a great time she had with him. "He is hung like a horse" is what she said and that of course piqued my interest. I hadn't played with a big one for several years and I was more than ready for some fun with someone who had some size to him so I flirted with Sean off and on and then the personal assistant's job opened up and I put on a full court press until he asked me to have dinner with him.

All it was supposed to be was me sounding him out and deciding whether or not he could be discrete. Curse the bad luck that I was seen holding hands with him although I sincerely doubt that I was looking at him 'dreamy eyed.' Not touching up my lipstick was a major mistake, but I only kissed Sean once when he walked me to my car so I didn't expect that my make up would be all that smudged. But it was a hell of a kiss and it had me up on the toes of my high heels. I was probably going to have to cancel my long lunch date with him; at least until I got things squared away with Rob and getting him past his snit fit.

As I fell asleep my last thought was that dinner with Sean hadn't been worth the crap I was getting from my husband.

***

She was dressed for work and was fixing breakfast when I came into the kitchen. The coffee was made and I poured myself a cup and added cream and sugar.

"Don't make any for me. I'll catch a bite at the diner near work."

"You are being silly Rob; there is no need for you to go to a diner and spend money when we already have breakfast here."

"At the diner I won't have to sit on the other side of the table and look at you. Don't bother on figuring on me for dinner either. The less of you I see the better I'm going to like it."

"Damn it Rob; you aren't being fair. All it was was dinner with a friend."

"Then you can have dinner with him again tonight since I won't be here."

"God damn it Rob; be reasonable. It was only a dinner date with a co-worker."

"The trouble Beverly is that I have been too damned reasonable for too damned long."

I left the house and headed for the diner. I got to work forty minutes later and since I was a half hour early I got on the Net and started looking for apartments close to work. I found several in my price range and I made a list. I'd start checking them out on my lunch hours. My goal was to be out of the house in two weeks.

Bev could have the house. I never wanted the damned thing to begin with. It had too much yard, was in what I considered the wrong neighborhood and was more than I could really afford. It was just one more thing that I had given in to Bev on. I loved the stupid cunt and wanted her to be happy so she usually got what she wanted. She could have the stupid fucking Lexus that she 'just had to have' and all the other shit she had talked me into getting. She could have it all as long as I got what I wanted – OUT!

At lunch time I hit the bank and cleaned out the savings account and took half of the checking account. I cashed in the nine certificates of deposit that were in the safe deposit box. I knew we would end up fighting over the funds and that she would probably get half, but I decided that I'd rather have the money and have her fight me for it than for her to have it and it being me fighting for it.

Back at work I got on the phone and called the credit card companies. I found out that it would be simpler to cancel the cards outright and have new ones issued in my name only than to have our current ones changed to my name only. It meant being card less for a couple of days while waiting for the new ones to arrive, but I could live with that.

Just before I left work that day I stopped by the boss's office and told him I was going to be going through a divorce and that he could expect that I'd be taking some time off of work to see attorneys, go to court and the like. He was understanding and only asked that I give him as much advance notice as I could as to when I'd be off.

I left work and hit the Outback Steak House for dinner and then stopped at Bud's Bar for a beer or two. Brandy set the PBR down in front of me and asked:

"Why the glum look Rob?"

Brandy and I went way back. We had gone to school together and I was very good friends with her and her husband Sam and I got to be the shoulder she cried on when she lost Sam to cancer. As I sipped my PBR I told her the story or at least as much of it as I was willing to share.

"Any chance the two of you can work it out?"

"I very much doubt it."

"So I might get my chance after all?"

"I beg your pardon?"

"Oh come on Rob; you have to know I had a crush on you all through school. It killed me when you never looked my way because you were so gaga over Beverly."

"Really? I guess you are right. I never noticed."

"Well keep me in mind if and when you cut loose from Bev."

Another customer called for her and she moved down the bar to take care of him. As she walked away I was smiling for the first time since Bev walked out the door to go to her dinner date. What Brandy had said was a big shot in the arm for me. Face it. What happened with Bev was a downer as far as my feelings of self worth were concerned. To have a beautiful woman tell me that she is interested in me was a hell of a pick up for the ego. The only problem was that Brandy had said "When you get loose from Bev" and I didn't see it happening for a while. I had decided against going for a divorce. Why waste the money on legal fees and court costs. I'd just walk away and move into an apartment or condo. Would Brandy still be interested in me under those circumstances?

I had one more beer and then headed on home or as it should now be called – the place where I was currently staying.

***

Beverly was sitting there waiting for me when I got there.

"Are you over your snit yet?"

"It isn't a snit Beverly. It is me deciding that I don't want anything to do with you."

"You are making a mountain out of a mole hill Rob."

"I don't think so Beverly. I'm looking at it as taking a bulldozer and cutting the mountain down to ground level."

She looked at me as if she didn't understand what I was saying, which she probably didn't, and then she said:

"I tried to use my Visa today and it was declined so I gave them my Discover card and it was declined also. I called and they told me the cards had been cancelled."

"Yep. It is one of the things to do when you separate."

"Separate? For God's sake Rob, it was only a dinner!"

"So you say, but I don't believe it and you are wasting my time and yours by continuing to say it. Now if you will excuse me I brought some contracts home that I have to review" and I walked away from her and into the den.

I was sitting at the desk going over the Snelling contract and making notes on some things that needed to be changed or clarified when Beverly came into the room.

"We have to have a serious talk Rob. Things are getting way out of hand here."

I put the contract down and turned to face her.

"You want a serious conversation Beverly? Well just sit your ass down and we will have one. I'll start it by saying that you are a lying, cheating slut and I have always known it. I knew it when I married you.

Did you think that I didn't know what you were doing when we were dating? I damned sure did, but I put it down as you spreading your wild oats while you were still single. I thought, or maybe hoped, that you would get it out of your system and settle down and be a faithful wife, but we both know that wasn't the case don't we?

"You have no idea how many of my friends and even some people that I didn't know very well tried to talk me out of marrying you, but I was in love and I thought you loved me enough to honor your vows once we were married. Again, we both know how that worked out. You are probably not aware of it, but you have a certain aura about you when you have been fucked. I always knew when you cheated on me because I could see it on you. I put up with it because you never did it except when I was out of town. When I was home you were affectionate and loving so I convinced myself that you did love me, but were some kind of a nymphomaniac and needed more than I could give you. I figured that I could live with it as long as you loved me.

"Then along came Gary. Oh yes Beverly; I knew all about Gary. I don't know how it started, but I knew it was happening. Did you know that Gary liked to brag about the women he was fucking? Well he did and it eventually got back to me and for the first time I began to doubt that you loved me. As your affair with him went on and on I decided that you were going to leave me for him so I didn't call you on it. The commissions I made on the trips he sent me on to get me out of the way so he could fuck you went into an account at another bank and they were going to be my slush fund when you left me. Confronting you over Gary would have ended those trips and I needed those commissions.

"I was surprised when Gary left and you didn't go with him. Did you know that he was a victim of a hit and run? He was walking down the street and a car jumped the curb and hit him and then drove away. He lost both legs and is confined to a wheelchair. I think it happened about the time I went out to LA to visit my sister.

"It wasn't until after Gary was gone that I found out about his large cock. One of the guys in the office wondered out loud if Gary was still able to use his large cock now that he was stuck in a wheelchair. It was then that I decided that maybe you were one of those size queens I'd heard about. I decided that you probably loved his dick and not him and I relaxed. You were still loving and affectionate and life fell back into the familiar pattern of you only fucking when I was out of town.

"And just so you know, since Sarah was conceived during your affair with Gary I had a DNA test done and just for giggles and grins I had one done on Billy too. I'm sure that you will be surprised to know that both of them are mine.

"I've lived with it all these years Beverly because I have loved you since the day we met and I thought you loved me. Right now you are asking yourself "If that is the way it has been and he has known all along why is he so bent out of shape now?" The reason is simple Beverly. Before you thought you were being discrete and making sure that I never found out. Kind of like living a separate life when I wasn't around, but this time was a flat out, in your face "I'm going out with another man. The total disrespect you showed me in doing that showed me what you really thought of me. You never loved me. I was just someone to fill up your time between lovers; a clueless twit that you felt safe having around.

"You didn't even try to hide what you did the other night. You could have dressed down and told me that you were having dinner with some of the girls from work, but you didn't do that. Oh no! You dressed your sexiest and let me know that it was a man you were going to be with. Then when I let you know how I felt about it did you reconsider? Hell no. Basically what you did was say:

"Fuck you Rob; I'm going!"

"I hope you enjoyed your date Beverly because I would hate to think you didn't considering what it cost you. You pissed your marriage away Beverly. The clueless safe husband that you used to have is now history. Okay Beverly. You wanted to have a serious talk so go ahead. What do you want to talk about?"

***

I was stunned. I didn't know what to say. Rob wasn't supposed to know any of those things. I'd been so careful to hide things so he would never find out. I could see now that dinner with Sean was a huge mistake. I'd taken Rob for granted for so long that I didn't think through. What the hell was I to do now?

Regardless of what Rob thought I did love him and I didn't want to lose him, but unless I could convince him of that he was gone. Given how much he seemed to know I knew that the truth was my only chance. If I could make him see that it wasn't lack of love for him that had me doing what I did I might have a chance. After all, he did stay with me even knowing what he knew. I took a deep breath and then said:

"You are absolutely wrong Rob. I do love you and I do respect you and I'm sorry that it has gotten to where you don't think I do. I know it is my own fault that you are thinking that, but nothing is farther from the truth. Yes, I have done all the things you mentioned, but none of it was done because I didn't love you. I only did it when you were out of town and not just because it was easier to hide things from you, but because when you were home you were all that I wanted.

"You are right in both of your assumptions. I am somewhat of a nymphomaniac and I am a size queen. Gary was never a threat to you. All he had going for him was eleven inches and you would have to be a woman to understand the attraction to that large of a cock. None of the men I spent time with were anything more to me than human dildos. It was sex they gave me.

"Your trips are always a week long. When you are home do we ever go two nights without making love? No we didn't and it was because I couldn't go that long without it. There wasn't any way I could go a full week without it. Think about it Rob. Almost thirty years together and we are still making love three, four and five times a week.

Ask our married friends how their sex lives are and I'll bet once or twice every two weeks is the best they do. So yes, I am some kind of nympho.

"Sean was a mistake. I could have – should have – handled it better."

Even though I had already decided that the truth would be my best shot I did have to tell Rob a small lie.

"I did not leave the house planning on having sex with Sean. He is the VP of Sales and he is looking for a personal assistant. I want the job and I let him know it. He asked me to have dinner with him so we could talk about it in a social setting instead of in the office where we would be constantly interrupted. I dressed my best to show him a side of me that he's never seen in the office. I felt that necessary since part of the job as his assistant would be to attend meetings and social functions with him when he called on clients and I wanted him to know that he wouldn't have to be ashamed of being seen with me.

"Was I trying to entice him? No lies here Rob; I was. I wanted that job. Would we have ended up in bed if I had gotten it? Very likely. He is reputed to be very large, but I wouldn't fuck him to get the job. After I had the job and had settled into it it very likely would have happened. To be perfectly honest about it even if I didn't get the job sooner or later if probably would have happened. After all, I am a girl who likes size and I would have eventually wanted to see what he had, but again, no way would I go to bed with him just to get the job.

"Honest to God Rob, it was only dinner and it was never meant to be anything but dinner. I do love you and disrespecting you was the farthest thing on my mind."

"So did you get the job?"

"I doubt it. He did hint that my being accommodating would go a long way toward helping him make a decision in my favor. I let him know that I wouldn't do anything in appropriate just to get the job."

"But you also let him know that somewhere down the line he might get lucky?"

"I may have hinted at it."

"So you are going to fuck him eventually."

"Of course not. I can't now."

"What makes you say that?"

"The fact that you know what you know. I don't know if I can hang on to you or not, but I have to try and that means I'm going to have to change."

"Bullshit Beverly! You have already said it yourself. You are a nymphomaniac and a size queen. Even if we stayed together sooner or later the opportunity to try out his big cock would be there and you would convince yourself that since I've known what you have been doing for years once more wouldn't hurt. Besides, you would convince yourself that you could hide it since I still take trips for the company. You would do it on my first or second day gone figuring that the aura I told you about would have faded by the time I got home."

"No I wouldn't Rob. I'll do whatever I have to do to keep you even to the point of quitting my job if I have to. I'll change Rob. I swear to God I will change."

"Twenty-three years of marriage, four years of college and the last two years of high school add up to twenty-nine years of being a cock hungry slut and you want me to believe that you can instantly change? No way Beverly; no fucking way!"

"I can do it Rob. Give me a chance. I know I can do it."

***

I looked at her and wondered if she could. I loved her; always had and probably always would. I'd lived with what she was for the entire time I'd known her so could I take the chance?

"I don't know Beverly. I'm going to have to think on it."

"Just give me a chance Rob. That's all I'm asking, just give me a chance."

"I'll think on it, but for now I need to get back to reviewing this contract" and I turned back to the desk. She sat there and quietly watched me for a few minutes and then she got up and left the room.

I did think about it over the next couple of days and it always came back to the fact that I loved Beverly and I always would. Could she change? Could a leopard change its spots? I knew that if I gave in Beverly would cheat again. It was in her makeup – it was part of who she was. She might try; she might try hard, but there was no doubt in my mind that down the road the Sean guy with the reputed large horn was going to get a taste of Beverly. She would try to hide it, but I'd know. I always knew. I'd known it for over twenty-nine years and I'd lived with it just so I could have Beverly. I'd only blown my stack because I'd seen what she had done as a slap in the face; a "Fuck you Rob. I don't care if you like it or not I'm going to do it."

After a couple of days of rolling it over in my mind I made a decision. Maybe not the best one, but one I could live with. The question was could Beverly live with it? She was used to my being accommodating to her every wish and whim and I do admit to being a bit of a wimp where she was concerned. I loved her so much and wanted her to be happy so I gave in almost any time she wanted something. After so many years could she accept that it wasn't going to be that way anymore if I stayed?

When I got home from work Friday I found Beverly dressed basically the same as she had been dressed on the night of her 'date' with Sean. I was a bit sarcastic when I said:

"Another date with Sean?"

"No Rob; not this time. You said that this is the way I usually dress when I expect us to end up in bed making love. I'm dressed this way because I want to go out and celebrate my new job and then come home and show you how much I want you."

I had decided to come home and lay down the new ground rules of how things were going to be if I stayed, but her news changed that. I didn't want to ruin her happy mood so I said:

"Give me a minute to change and I'll be right with you."

We had dinner at Antonio's and I let her monopolize the conversation. She had talked to Sarah that afternoon and she brought me up to date on what was going on with my daughter and she told me all about what she would be doing in her new job. We left the restaurant and went to the Black Mushroom for drinks and dancing. There was more general conversation when we sat and drank between dances, but neither of us touched on our current situation.

On the drive home she happily told me what she planned to do with the increase in her paycheck that the new job would bring. Things didn't get tense until we got home. Obviously she wanted me to join her in the bedroom and just as obviously she was on pins and needles to see what I was going to do. She was hoping that I wouldn't say "Goodnight" and head for Sarah's bedroom. She was surprised when I told her to have a seat on the couch while I paid a visit to the bathroom. When I came into the living room she was sitting there looking apprehensive. I sat down opposite her and said:

"Over the last few days I've spent a lot of time thinking on our situation and on where I wanted to go and what I wanted to do."

Her face fell as she braced herself for bad news.

"It hasn't been easy coming to a decision because regardless of which way I go there are too many things over which I have no control so I have decided that I'm going to stay with you."

Her face brightened at that and I went on.

"But there are going to be some major changes to the way that things have been. I am no longer going to be a doormat for you. The days of me letting you have your way just so I could see you happy are gone. There are some things that I've always wanted to do but didn't because you didn't want to and again I didn't push because I wanted you to be happy and also – to be brutally honest – because of all the fucking around you did I wasn't all that secure and I was afraid that if I pushed you might leave me for one of your lovers. Now that I've found that I'm strong enough to walk away from you that is no longer a worry.

"You do have some say in the matter, but I'll tell you up front that a "no" from you will have me heading suitcase in hand for the door. It shouldn't be any big thing for you since I'm willing to bet all that I have that you have done it for your lovers. From now on when you suck my cock you will let me cum in your mouth if I want to and you will swallow. Understand?"

She nodded a yes and I said, "The other thing is that you are going to let me tap that ass you have kept me away from since we first started having sex. These things are non-negotiable. As I said, you do have a choice in the matter. You can say no and that you don't want things to go that way and you already know what the consequences will be if you refuse. So, the choice is yours. What's it going to be?"

She sat there looking at me and I wondered what was going on in her head and then she smiled and said:

"We don't have any KY, but there is Crisco in the pantry. I'm going up to the bedroom. Do you want me to leave the heels on or take them off?"

The Crisco was a little messy and I made a mental note to get some KY. Maybe a gallon to start.

***

The one thing we never discussed was her penchant for extracurricular sexual activities. I was a realist. She either would or she wouldn't, but if she did and it wasn't an "In your face" occurrence and she hid it from me (or tried to) I probably wouldn't say anything. What the hell, she'd done it for the entire time we had been together and I'd known and lived with it.

Sometimes it really sucks what you are willing to do out of love.

End of the 8th Story

What Would I Do Without Leslie

I remember the day and the time. It was the day of my thirty-fifth birthday and the time was 5:26 am. I know because I saw the clock when I reached over and silenced the alarm. I looked over at Leslie who would stay in bed another hour and saw something that I hadn't noticed before. Her night gown had slid down and I saw a love bite - a small hickey - on the underside of her left breast. And I had not been the one to put it there. I have at times put love bites on my wife so I knew how long it usually took them to fade and that told me that the one on her breast was recent.

My wife was cheating on me!

As I sat there on the edge of the bed and stared at the mark on her breast I thought back trying to think of any signs that might indicate how long she had been doing it, but I couldn't think of a thing. I hadn't noticed any lack of affection on her part or any changes in her behavior. Well, there was one small change; she was usually all over me when I got home from one of my frequent business trips, but when I'd returned the day before she hadn't. She said she really wanted to, but it was her time of the month.

At the time she told me that I had just accepted it as a fact of life, but looking at that obscene thing on her left tit I had to ask myself if she was really on the rag or just using it as an excuse so that she wouldn't have to get naked with me. Like most men I didn't keep track of my wife's cycle; I just kept on keeping on until she said, "Sorry honey, but I'm out of commission for a while."

Well, I thought as I got off the bed and headed for the bathroom, at least now I know why she didn't answer the phone when I had called her on the two nights I spent in Chicago. Out being busy with her lover or not brave enough to reach over and pick up the bedside phone while he was there in bed with her.

And then I started thinking on what I was going to do about it. Immediate confrontation was out! I was going to want to know who, where and how often and I obviously could not trust her to tell me and be truthful. Confrontation would only cause her to deny things and come up with some excuse for why the mark was there and then quit or slow down on what she was doing. Nope. No confrontation till I had all the facts. And then? Good question I thought; damned good question.

***

Leslie and I went all the way back to grade school. We were the same age so we were in the same classes. Her last name was Taylor and mine was Talbot and in the early grades since the teachers usually had you sit in alphabetical order we usually ended up sitting next to each other.

The alphabet thing threw us together for a lot of activities like the time in the seventh grade when during Phys Ed they gave us dance classes and Leslie ended up as my partner. In the eighth grade we had a teacher who was big on class projects and she was always breaking us up into groups. Naturally she did it alphabetically so Leslie and I usually ended up together there also.

All of that alphabetically caused closeness had a far reaching effect that I did not realize until much later. Somewhere along the line that closeness gave Leslie the idea we were meant to be together - that I was supposed to be her boyfriend. Girls started thinking about things like that earlier than boys do. I had no interest in girls until I hit the ninth grade and when I did start to notice girls Leslie wasn't one of them.

The first girl to cause my heart to speed up was Pauline French. I dated her twice before she started turning me down when I asked her out. I was crushed - for all of two weeks - and then I went after Nancy Wilde. I had three dates with Nancy before she started putting me off when I asked for a date. After Nancy there were a half dozen others who would go out with me once or twice and then not have anything more to do with me. I moved into the tenth grade thinking that I had a bad case of body odor and really bad breath. I couldn't understand it because I took regular baths and brushed my teeth two or three times a day.

Our school had a dance once a month on a Friday night. Not a prom type dance, just a dance designed to help kids learn to socialize (and keep them off the streets on a Friday night). You could go to it stag and dance with the girls who came alone or you could take a date. Going stag marked you as "lame" and most guys did not want that tag hung on them so if they couldn't get a date they didn't go.

It was the third week of the tenth grade and the dance was the coming Friday. I had been turned down by four girls and had decided not to go when Leslie leaned over to me in Civics class and asked me who I was taking to the dance. Rather than admit that I couldn't get a date I just said that I hadn't planned on going. Then she asked me if I would do her a favor. I asked her what and she wanted to go to the dance, but that she really wasn't interested in any of the guys who had asked her.

"Would you take me Rob? I'd really like to go."

I'm not sure why, but I am guessing that my constant closeness to Leslie had me looking at her more like a sister or something like that, maybe a "not seeing the tree because of the forest" thing. I pulled back and took a good look at Leslie and suddenly wondered why I hadn't been paying attention to her. She was a great looking girl!

I told her that I would like very much to take her to the dance and that was the start of it. I had a great time at the dance and when I walked her to her door when I took her home she kissed me. I asked her if she would like to go to the movies with me on Saturday and she said yes and from then on we were a couple.

Most people could not understand it since Leslie and I were as different as night and day. We were oil and water and everyone knows that the two don't mix, but somehow we did. I was a quiet, unassuming guy and my after school activities were things like the Chess Club, the History Club and the jazz and classical music clubs. Leslie was an outgoing, aggressive over-achiever. She was on the cheer leading squad and played soccer and field hockey.

Looking back at it now I guess that it was maybe six months into our relationship that Leslie started running my life. It was so subtle that I never even noticed. In fact it wasn't even something that I realized until after I started looking into Leslie's cheating. It was little things like, "Oh no Rob, that tie just isn't right for you" and telling me that the barber that I had used for years "was just butchering my hair. You need to go to Anton's."

The biggest thing she did to me way back when was to get me to go out for a sport - any sport at all.

"It makes me look bad to the other girls on the squad (meaning the other cheerleaders) to have a boyfriend who isn't into sports."

I wanted to please Leslie so I went out for football and I even made the team and played varsity in the eleventh and twelfth grades. I wasn't any good and I knew it. For one thing I was too slow. For another at 6'2'' and 165 pounds I lacked the beef to be able to block for beans, but I had one thing going for me - my hands. If the quarterback could get the ball to me I would catch it. I couldn't go anywhere with it after I caught it, but then I really didn't need to, Third and twelve and I'd go down fifteen yards and if Jason could get the ball anywhere close to me I'd catch it, get tackled, but we still have the first down. Coverage didn't matter. Get it to me and I'd catch it.

When football was over I tried basketball. But was just too clumsy. I tried baseball, but pretty much sucked at it. Again, too slow and I could never hit the ball. Track and field was out - the slow thing again - but then a coach suggested wrestling. My weight put me in a class where anyone else who was that weight was smaller, height wise than me, and my 6'2" against their 5'9" or 5'10" gave me what amounted to a four inch reach advantage. I wasn't all that great as a wrestler, but I did well enough to letter in it.

Two other areas where Leslie worked on me were education and sex. I intended to get a degree in Business Management and then go on and get an MBA. When we started eleventh grade Leslie began pushing computer science.

"You don't want to be a stodgy old businessman honey. Put that fantastic mind of yours to good use. Information technology is the wave of the future."

By the time I graduated she had managed to talk me into computers.

And then there was sex!

With my upbringing I had the mindset that you abstained until you were married. Leslie was having none of that. It made for an awkward situation. Every other guy I knew was in a constant hunt for a willing girl while I was doing my best to hold Leslie off. We had hot - very hot - necking sessions, but every time Leslie's hands would wander I would push them away and tell her that we needed to wait.

"But I don't want to wait. I'm ready now."

I mentioned she was aggressive didn't I? We were at the lake on a Saturday. It was just turning dark and I was lying on a blanket when Leslie came out of the water and dropped down next to me. "I hope that you are not too worn out" she said and then she jerked my swimming trunks down and took my cock in her mouth before I even knew what was happening. I went to push her away and she clenched her jaw and I felt her teeth close on my cock and I wisely stopped trying to shove her away. She relaxed her jaw muscles and proceeded to give me my first ejaculation that wasn't by my own hand.

I was amazed when she kept her mouth on me and swallowed all of my discharge. She licked my cock clean and then went back to sucking on it until it was hard again. Once I was up again she moved on top of me and guided me into her as she pushed herself down. Once she had me in her she began to rock back and forth and she looked down at me and smiled.

"I told you that I didn't want to wait."

It wasn't until I dropped her off at her house that it dawned on me that Leslie was not a virgin when I slid into her. She had some experience and I wondered where she had gotten it, but not enough to ask her. From that day on Leslie and I made love whenever we got the chance.

There were a lot of other changes, too many to mention here, but by the time we were halfway through our freshman year in college Leslie was pretty much running my life. Not that I noticed at the time and not that I would have cared. Why would I? Things were going good so why would I have cared even if I had noticed. I didn't even think twice about it when someone did tell me that I was being manipulated.

It was at a kegger at one of the frat houses. I was sipping a beer when Nancy Wilde came up to me and asked me why she had never heard from me again. I told her that after being turned down by her a half a dozen time it was obvious to me that she wasn't interested.

"Well that wasn't exactly true Rob. I was interested, but I was scared off and now it seems that I was lied to."

"I don't understand."

"I was told that I should stay away from you because you had a social disease. Gonorrhea is what I think she said."

"Who the hell told you that?"

"Your girlfriend."

"Leslie? How would she know even if it were true? I didn't start dating her until well after I stopped seeing you."

"What she said was that her cousin worked in the office of the doctor that you see and her cousin told her that she had seen the results of a test that you took. I don't know what she told the other girls that scared them away, but what she told me scared me away. Then, when no one else would go out with you, she moved in. She must love you a lot to go to all that trouble."

And that is what I keyed in on - "She must love you a lot" - and I never mentioned the conversation to Leslie.

***

Mid junior year Leslie asked me if I had given any thought to our wedding. Did I want it big with all the hoopla or small and quiet? That caught me off guard because I hadn't even proposed. Not that I didn't love her, it was just that I assumed that we would always be together and I assumed she felt the same way so I had never bothered to formalize things. I thought about her question for a moment or so and then told her that I didn't have a preference so I would leave it up to her to do whatever she wanted. From the smile I got I assumed that it was the right answer and two days later she told me that her mother was starting to work on the planning and Leslie suggested a date six months after graduation and I said that it was okay by me.

Three months before graduation I started sending out resumes and I received several responses. One night I was sorting through them trying to decide which ones I wanted to interview for and in what order when Leslie handed me one that she had been reading and said:

"Here honey; this one is perfect for you."

My attitude was simply "I'm about ready to graduate and I need a job" and it didn't really matter to me who I was working for as long as I was working. I arranged an interview with the XYZ Corporation (the one Leslie picked) and they made me an offer and I took it and the wedding (full blown, church and reception) took place in February.

Looking back on my life as I pondered Leslie's cheating I was astounded at how much she had controlled me without me ever realizing it. In my defense I can only say that every decision made for us by Leslie was on something that I didn't care much about one way or the other. She picked out the house we bought, what we furnished it with, the cars we drove and on and on and on. I didn't care because everything she did was something I didn't have to do. As far as the house was concerned all I cared about was a roof over my head. House, condo or apartment, I didn't care. Cars? As long as it got me where I wanted to go I didn't care what kind it was. I had pretty much turned everything over to Leslie.

I worked hard at XYZ and over the years I was promoted several times until I became the manager of Information Services and in addition I was the company's lead trouble-shooter on IT problems. Since XYZ was a national company with offices in several cities I was traveling on the average of ten days out of the month. Leslie rose in her company and eventually reached the position of regional manager which meant that she also had to travel to visit the offices in her region.

Leslie had some leeway as to when she had to visit the offices in her region so she tried to schedule her visits to coincide with the times I would be on the road. It wasn't always possible though since my trips were usually because of an IT emergency that had just occurred but we were still able to spend more time with each other than two people with traveling jobs should have been able to.

For sixteen years I had honestly believed that I had the perfect wife and the ideal marriage and it was a hell of a shock to me to find out that I was wrong.

***

I was gone before Leslie got out of bed and I suppose that was a good thing because I'm not sure that I could have kept it together if I would have had to face her that morning. I spent the ride to work wondering just what I would have to do to find out the who, when and where. Eventually I would also probably want to know why, but that could wait.

I did know one thing though and that was that I was going to need some legal advice. I got out the Yellow Pages when I got to work and looked under the listings for attorneys for one who specialized in divorces and while I had the book open I also checked out private detectives. I was reaching for the phone when it suddenly occurred to me that I couldn't call an attorney or an investigator just then. I would need to pay them and Leslie handled the family finances and she would see it right away and then we would have the confrontation that I wasn't ready for. Unless I could come up with some funds that Leslie didn't know about I would have to hold off. I needed something positive before I could go to either one. Once I knew for sure I could go to the detective and have him nail it down and then I could go to a lawyer. Then if Leslie caught the expenditures and the confrontation occurred I would be on firm ground. There was no other way - I was going to have to follow Leslie and spy on her until she gave me something concrete.

You will note that nowhere have I mentioned sitting down and trying to talk things out and maybe finding a way to get the marriage back working. No sir, wasn't going to happen. She was either mine or she wasn't and if she wasn't she was gone.

I did have a small stroke of luck. At eleven in the morning Leslie called me. One of her offices had been broken into and she was going to have to catch a flight and she would be gone at least overnight. That meant that I wouldn't have to face her for at least another twenty-four hours. Maybe by the next time I saw her face to face I would have myself under control and be able to hide the fact that I was onto her.

If I had not seen that love bite what happened next would never have happened.

Since Leslie was going to be out of town I decided to stop at the Starlight, a lounge where the group that Leslie and I hung with, usually congregated. I walked into the place and looked around and saw a dozen or so people that I knew and suddenly I just felt like I really didn't want to be around anyone. What I really needed was to be alone. I turned around and went back out to the parking lot and got in my car. I was just pulling out of the lot when I felt the need to go to the bathroom. I pulled over and went in the back door and down the short hallway and into the men's room.

I was sitting in one of the stalls when someone came in and I heard him unzip and start to take a whiz. The door opened and someone else came in and I heard a voice that I recognized as Brad Brown's say:

"Did you see Talbot come in?"

"Yeah. I wonder what's up with that?" Chris Chambers said.

"He looked around and probably realized that every guy he saw had been fucking his wife."

There was a lot of laughter and then Brown said, "Do you really think he knows?"

"No idea, but as much as she fucks around on him I don't see how he couldn't at least suspect something."

"Maybe he is one of those guys who get off on knowing his wife is a slut."

"Rob? No fucking way. Not Mr. Straight Arrow."

"You tap her lately?"

"Two days ago when he was in Chicago. He made his nightly check in phone call and she was reaching for the phone when I stopped her. I was too damned close to getting off to slow down while she talked to him. I think it pissed her off. I think she gets off on talking to him while some other guy is fucking her."

"No, that's not it. She did it one time when I was fucking her and I asked her that very question and she looked at me like I was some kind of freak and said no, that she loved him and just wanted to hear the sound of his voice."

"You get any of her lately?"

"Not lately. I haven't been lucky enough to be in here when she's come looking for a playmate."

I heard both of them zip up and Brown was saying as they walked out, "Maybe you should just call her and have her set up one of those fake out of to…" and the door closing cut off the rest of what he was saying.

Fake out of town trips? Is that where she was right then? Not on a trip to an office that had been broken into, but in a hotel or motel right here in town fucking some asshole?

I thought about the men I'd seen when I walked into the lounge. They were all supposed to be my friends, but Chambers said that everyone that I saw had been fucking my wife. When I left home that morning I thought that I was as bummed as I could get, but things had just gotten worse -- a whole lot worse. A faithless wife and now friends who were stabbing me in the back.

***

I was in bed when she called. "Hi honey. Miss me?"

As I lied to her and told her that I did I wondered if she was on a bed with a cock in her.

"I wish I was home honey, I miss you when you aren't around."

I'll just bet I thought as I said, "I don't sleep well when you aren't around either."

"I should only be here one day baby and you had better conserve your energy because I'll be more than ready when I get home."

And at that moment I knew that I wasn't going to be home when she got there. Our Denver office was going to have an emergency and I would be on a road trip. I would rent a motel room and then follow her while she thought that I was out of town. According to what I'd heard from Brown and Chambers Leslie played while I was on my trips. I'd fake a three day trip and see for myself.

The next day I had a long talk with my boss. I told him what was going on and that I was going to need to take a couple of days off. I called Leslie on her cell and told her that the system in Denver had crashed and I had to catch a flight. She whined that she was so looking forward to seeing me and couldn't I put the trip off for at least a day and of course I told her that it would be impossible for me to do that and that I'd see her in three days.

As I hung up it occurred to me that I didn't have a clue as to how I was going to follow Leslie when she came home. Would she go straight from the airport to the lounge? Would she call one of her fuck buddies and drive from the airport to his place or meet him at a motel? Would she go to her office first and then go meet her lover (or lovers) or would she drive straight home, unpack, shower and then go out or would her lover of the moment meet her at our house? And then of course there was the possibility that she was still in town - that her trip had been a fake - and she would just stay where she was with whoever it was she was fucking.

I could have driven out to the airport and looked for her car, but I didn't think I would have a prayer of finding it among the thousands of cars spread between eight different parking lots and what if she had used one of the satellite parking companies that bus you to the terminal? I finally decided that all I could do was park somewhere in the neighborhood where I could watch the house and wait for her to come home.

She pulled into the drive at 5:10 and once in the garage I saw her get a small suitcase out of the trunk of her car and then the garage door closed. It was another four hours before the garage door opened again and Leslie backed down the drive. I gave her a two block head start and then I followed along behind her. I did it pretty much the way I had seen it done on the cop shows - always keeping at least two cars between us - and I wasn't all that surprised when she pulled into the parking lot at the Starlight.

She parked and I saw her put her cell phone up to her ear. Aha, I thought, going to call her lover and let him know she was at the lounge and waiting for him. Almost immediately my cell phone chirped and I answered it and Leslie said:

"Hi honey, it is just me."

"Are you home yet or still traveling?"

"You already know the answer to that one. I'd ask you how the weather is in Denver, but you wouldn't know that since you aren't in Denver. Why are you following me Rob?"

Well, there it was -- confrontation time. No use avoiding it anymore so I might as well just get it over with.

"I wanted to try and catch you with one of your legion of lovers."

"And why would you want to do that?"

"Morbid curiosity. See which one of my many so called friends would be stabbing me in the back tonight. Give me something to seethe about when I sit across the desk from the divorce lawyer."

"I can see that we need to talk. Why don't you run along home. I will be along shortly and we will talk."

"Run along home and you'll be along shortly? You aren't coming home now?"

"No I'm not. I came down here for a drink or two and I'm going to do just that."

"Then I'll come in and join you."

"Not after what you just told me. I need to unwind after my trip and loosen up some and I do not want you sitting there trying to drag me down. I'll see you at home."

She disconnected and got out of her car and without even looking my way she walked into the Starlight. Didn't want me bringing her down? In less than forty-eight hours she had turned my life inside out and upside down and she didn't want me around to drag her down? I had my hand on the door handle getting ready to open the door, get out and follow her in when I stopped myself. I was not a believer in airing dirty laundry in public and if Chris and Brad were telling the truth, and I had no reason to doubt them, the place would be packed with all of my ex-friends who were her fuck buddies and I just didn't feel like embarrassing myself in front of all of them. The last thing I needed right then was a bunch of people that I knew laughing at me.

I started up, pulled out of the lot and headed home. I got about two blocks and then on an impulse I turned around and went back. I parked on the side street where I could see Leslie's car and I didn't think she would notice me. I only had a fifteen minute wait before she came out of the lounge with Chris Chambers. I guess he was finally lucky enough to be in the lounge when Leslie came looking for a playmate. Or unlucky enough, depending on your point of view.

They got in his car and pulled out of the lot. I didn't bother to try and follow them because there was only one motel in the direction they were headed. I gave them five minutes and then drove to the Holiday Inn Express just down the street. I cruised the parking lot and saw the car parked there and then I left.

***

The car pulled into the driveway and stopped. The door opened and I came out from behind the bushes and swung the tire iron hard into the small of his back. Chris screamed as he went to his knees and my second swing caught his mouth and I saw teeth fly out. I kicked him in the chest and he fell onto his back and then I gave both of his knees several hard whacks with the tire iron. He was crying and moaning in pain when I grabbed a handful of his hair and pulled his face up close to mine.

"Was it fun fucking my wife tonight? You were supposed to be my friend asshole and you stabbed me in the back by fucking my wife. You have one chance and only one chance to keep this tire iron from turning your balls into mush. One lie, one untruthful answer and you will never have another hard on in this life. How long have you been fucking my wife?"

"Don't hit me anymore." He sobbed.

"Then answer the question."

"Five or six years."

"Why?"

"Because she wanted it. She came after me."

"Why?"

"I dunno. I guess it was just my turn."

"Your turn?"

"She was doing everybody else and I guess she just looked at me and decided that I was next."

"Who else has been fucking her that you know of?"

"Oh God, I don't know. Everybody."

"Give me names Chris. Give me the names of the ones you know for sure."

He rattled off a dozen or so names, all of them supposed friends. I shook my head in disgust.

"Here's the deal Chris. So far as I'm concerned we are even. You fucked me and so I fucked you up. You call the cops and when they get done with me I'll come looking for you and use a tire iron to break your elbows, your wrists, your ankles and turn your cock and balls into scrap and then break every other bone I can. Take what you just got and live with it as the price you had to pay for stabbing me in the back or carry it farther and end up spending the rest of your life in a wheel chair with someone feeding you with a spoon. Again, your choice."

I walked away from him and left him moaning on the ground next to his car.

***

Leslie was home when I got there and it was obvious that she was upset because I hadn't been there patiently waiting for her.

"Where have you been?"

"Out taking care of some business."

"What kind of business would that be at this time of night?"

"None of yours."

She looked at me for several seconds and then shrugged and said, "All right Rob, what is this nonsense about divorce lawyers?"

"Not nonsense Leslie. Divorce lawyers are the people you end up doing business with when you find out that your wife is a cheating whore."

She looked at me for several more seconds and then said, "What has changed Rob? We have had a good marriage for over sixteen years. I've been a great wife to you and you have been happy so why do you want to end it now?"

"Because I found out about you and what you have been doing behind my back."

"So what Rob? I've been doing it for the entire sixteen years of our marriage and it hasn't affected the quality of your life one little bit. In fact, it has been even longer than sixteen years. I've had other lovers all the time we have been together from high school up till now and it hasn't hurt a thing."

"That long?"

"Yes Rob, that long and again, it has not hurt a thing."

"I'm that lacking in the bedroom?"

"You aren't lacking anything Rob. You do very well in the bedroom. In fact, you are head and shoulders above most of the others."

"Then why?"

"I like variety Rob. Big cocks, small cocks, black ones, white ones, Asian and Latino. I just like variety and I also need just a little more than you - or any other man for that matter - can give me. I only do it when I'm out of town or you are out of town so it won't interfere with our time together and again Rob, it has not hurt us one bit. Right now the only problem we have is that you have a bruised ego, but I will kiss it and make it better."

"I don't think so Leslie and it is a little bit more than a bruised ego. There is also the humiliation of knowing that all so my so called friends look at me and smirk to themselves knowing that they have fucked my wife and made me a cuckold. And as for you never doing it except when I'm out of town? I'm in town tonight and you still went to that motel with Chris and you did it knowing that I was following you to try and catch you doing just that.

"That shows me just what you really think of me. You think so little of me that you could say, "Just run along home," go to a motel and fuck another man and then come home and tell me that everything is just fine and that all it is, is that you just need a little variety and expect me to say, "Yes dear" and get on with life. It ain't gonna happen! No Leslie, the only reason our marriage was happy was because I didn't have a clue. But then I wasn't looking for one. I thought I had a perfect marriage and a loving wife, but I didn't and everyone knew it but me."

"You do have those things Rob. We do have a great marriage and you do have a loving wife."

"Maybe by your definition Leslie, but not by mine. Now if you will excuse me I need to go pack."

"Why? What are you going to do?"

"Leave your sorry ass, see an attorney and get on with my life."

"Don't be silly Rob. What on Earth will you do if I'm not there to guide you?"

"If you are not there to guide me?"

"Think back on it Rob. I'm the one who has made all the major decisions. Even as far back as high school I was the one who guided you along. You need me Rob."

"You really believe that?"

"Of course I do because it is true."

"If you believe that - really believe that- it changes things. You don't go out looking for other cocks because you like variety, you do it because you are looking for someone who you think is a man and you go looking for someone you think is manly because you think that I'm not. No real man would let a woman run his life for him would he? Any man who would let a woman do all of his thinking for him must be some namby-pamby wimp right? Well let me tell you something you cheating whore. The only thing you get credit for is for moving me from a career in Business Management to one in computers. All the rest of your big decisions were on things I didn't care enough about to get involved with and didn't give a rat's ass about. As far as I was concerned if you wanted them you could have them.

"It may have escaped you, but I have done extremely well in my career. You weren't in the office guiding me as I made decisions on what systems to use and how to set up the company's IT network. You weren't leaning over my shoulder guiding me when I went out to the customers and solved their problems. I did that on my own and without any help from you. But here is a news flash for you Leslie. Even if I couldn't make it without you to guide me I'd still be better off than I would be living with a round-heeled whore."

"It doesn't matter to you that I love you?"

"You don't love me Leslie and now I'm not sure that you ever did. You loved the idea of thinking you were controlling me; of thinking that I was your puppet. Well I've just cut the strings lady and you will need to go find someone else to dance as you pull the strings."

I packed enough to last me a few days and then left the house. I went back two days later when Leslie was at work and got everything else that I wanted out of the house. During that same two day period Brad Brown was attacked just outside his home on a dark night and both of his knees were wrecked by someone with a tire iron, baseball bat or some other heavy instrument. His attacker was masked and had never uttered a word as he beat on Brown. The police are still investigating.

When I told my boss I needed the time off to take care of personal problems I also told him what those problems were and asked him if he could arrange a transfer for me. I needed to get out of town and away from all of my so-called friends. I had the names from Chris of some of the ones who fucked Leslie, and I would get to them in time, but I didn't have the names of all the ones who had nailed the bitch and I didn't want to spend the rest of my life wondering if he "was one of them" every time I talked to some one that I knew. My boss arranged for me to move to our Kansas City office and I moved.

I never did see an attorney about a divorce. I'd let Leslie do it and pay for it. If she could. I cleaned out all of our accounts on the day that I left town. Only way she can get half back is to divorce me and then of course we would have to sell the house that she "just had to have."

I did have myself checked out for sexually transmitted diseases and I did triple the life insurance that I had on Leslie. Every night before I go to bed I pray for Leslie to get hit by a bus or be struck by lightning even though I know it is not likely to happen.

Leslie found out where I was and once a week she calls me and asks me if I'm over my "silly little snit fit" and ready to come home where I belong and every week she gets the same answer, "Fuck you" and a hung up phone.

Leslie is showing no signs of going for a divorce and I may have to rethink my position on letting her do it so she has to pay for it. I have met some very nice ladies in Kansas City and I just may need to get myself single again.

The End

Here is a sample from another story you may enjoy:

Just Plain Bob

7 INTENSE
STORIES IN 1

She
MAKES ME...

EROTICA SHORT STORIES, VOL. 16

What happened was Aimee. Aimee was the embodiment of the term 'California Beach Bunny'. Tall, tanned, long honey blond hair that hung to the middle of her back and a body built for the specific purpose of driving the male sex wild. Ted introduced us and then said, "Aimee and I are getting married."

Lucky bastard I thought even as I looked at her and thought that I had seen her someplace. You know how it is when you meet someone you think you've met before or seen some place? It crawls inside your head and stays with you as you drive yourself bananas trying to remember. She noticed my attention and she came over to me.

"Is there a sign on my back that says 'kick me' or are you staring at me because you are enthralled with my beauty?"

"Enthralled of course. That and the fact that I would swear on a stack of Bibles that I've seen you some place before now."

"When was the last time you were in California?"

"I've never been there."

"Well this is my first trip out of the state so I have no idea where we could have run across each other."

"Curious, but the feeling is there and it will eat on me until I resolve it, at least in my mind."

She shrugged and moved away to talk to somebody else and I went to find Teddy.

"Where are you staying while you are here?"

At the Best Western off Meadows and Founders Parkway."

"Bullshit bro. I'm sitting in an almost empty three-bedroom house and I could use the company. It gets lonely in that big place."

"Why don't you sell it? The place can't have much in the way of good memories for you."

"It is my revenge bro. The divorce decree gives Lisa half when I sell it, but not until I sell it and the decree doesn't set a time limit. If I live there for fifty years it means that cheating whore doesn't get a dime for fifty years. When we leave tonight we will swing by the Best Western and pick up your stuff. Tell Aimee not to worry. The house is so well built that it is almost sound proof. The two of you can raise all kinds of hell and I'll never hear a thing."

The party was running down and Ted and Aimee went to get

their coats and as we were heading for the door Aimee dropped her purse and bent down to pick it up. When she did her blouse rode up in the back and I saw the tattoo. It was intricate scrollwork about twelve inches long and maybe six inches high and as soon as I saw it the penny dropped and I knew where I had seen Aimee. I'd have to wait until I got home to make absolutely sure, but there really wasn't any doubt in my mind. When Aimee stood up she saw me looking at her and she read my facial expression and her facial expression told me what she saw – "He knows."

We made small talk on the way to the motel and then on the way to my house. Ted pointed out the local sites as we drove along, but Aimee was mostly quiet. She kept glancing over at me as if expecting that I would suddenly shout, "I know where it was that I saw you" and then proceed to tell Teddy. When we got to my place I showed them to their room and then I gave Aimee a tour of the place so she would know where to find things and then I bid them goodnight. I went to the living room and read until they had time to fall asleep and then I got up and headed for my home office. I booted up the computer, got on the Net and then logged onto one of my favorite sites. I went searching through the index until I found the section I was looking for, brought it up and there she was. Absolutely no doubt about it. The name on the clip was Lois, but it was sure enough Aimee.

I heard the door open and close behind me and I turned and saw Aimee standing there. "You know, don't you?"

I nodded a yes.

"All of it?"

Again I nodded a yes and pointed to the monitor where a clip from GangBang Squad was playing out. Aimee was on her knees inside a circle of five black men with large cocks and she was taking turns at sucking them. She looked over my shoulder, "I knew when I saw your face as we were leaving that you had figured it out. Not exactly my proudest moment."

"Maybe not, but you sure look good doing it."

"I was out of a job, the rent was due and I hadn't eaten in two days. I was really hurting for money when a guy I knew asked me if I would be interested in making fifteen hundred for something I usually did on weekend nights for free and I said yes. Only it wasn't like what I did on weekend nights. All I did then was pick out a cute guy and have some fun. I didn't know it was a bunch of black guys until I got there."

"Why didn't you leave?"

She shrugged, "I just said it. I was out of a job, the rent was due and I hadn't eaten in two days."

She pointed at the monitor, "You spend much time on that looking for porn?"

"Quite a bit. It is my sexual outlet since my wife left me for a couple of bikers."

"Then you will probably come across me again. After the gangbang I did a couple more to keep the money coming in until I could find a job. I did one for MILF Seekers, one for Her First Big Cock, one for Her First Anal and two for Suck Bus. You going to tell Teddy?"

"Of course not. He's happy, you seem happy, why should I screw things up for the two of you? I do have a question though."

"What?"

"I know how big Ted is in the cock department. You going to be happy with him in bed after all those huge cocks I've seen you take?"

"I won't lie. Big is good. Hell, big is great, but there is more to a marriage than just sex. Ted is very good in bed and as long as the love, affection, and caring are there what he has will be more than enough."

"Then I guess you should have a happy life because Ted has always given a hundred percent in everything that he does."

"Yes, well, I just have to make sure that he gets the chance to do it," she said as she moved toward me.

"What are you doing?"

"I'm not a very trusting person," she said as she took off her blouse.

If you enjoyed this sample then look for **She Makes Me…**.

Also by this Author:

The Prodigal Family: The Abbotts

Watching My Shared Wife

The Waitress and the Runaway Husband

Baiting Mr. Little

Too Hot for Henry

Chuck's Fantasy

The Redhead's Desires

Rescued at Riley's

His Every Fantasy

Open Mike Night

Pursuit for Revenge

Why Does He Do That?

Halloween & Drugs

Tracey

When Rob Met Kari

Becoming a Shared Wife, Vol. 1 –

(Wife Sharing and Other Adventures)

Becoming a Shared Wife, Vol. 2 –

(Hazardous Wives)

Becoming a Shared Wife, Vol. 3 –

(Wives Who Stray)

From the Author

WANT FREE COPIES OF MY BOOKS?

Just visit my blog and download free copies of my books:
awesomeauthors.org/justplainbob

If you enjoyed any of my books then please share the love and promote my books in Amazon.

If you write me a review and send me an email I will send you a free book, or many.
(Just know that these emails are filtered by my publisher.)

Good news is always welcome.

One Last Thing, For Kindle Readers...

When you turn the page, Kindle will give you the opportunity to rate this book and share your thoughts on Facebook and Twitter. If you enjoyed my writings, would you please take a few seconds to let your friends know about it? Because... when they enjoy they will be grateful to you and so will I.

Thank You!

An Open Letter from Just Plain Bob

A message for those who like my stories, those who hate my stories, those who are indifferent and those who have yet to make up their minds.

I have often stated that I really don't care what others think about my stories, that I write for my own enjoyment and then I offer to share. If you like my stories fine and if you don't, also fine since I have already satisfied my target audience - me!

It is human nature to strive to get better. If you take up bowling your first games are going low scoring, but you will work and practice to get better and as your average climbs you may forget the game where you had three gutter balls and shot an eighty-six, but that game is still there in your past.

Your first time on the golf course you shot an eighty on the front nine, but did you settle for that being your game or did you work to improve? You may eventually get a three handicap, but that nine hole eighty is still there as part of your past.

When you hired in at your job did you say, "Cool, I got it made" and do nothing more than what you barely had to do or did you go to work thinking that, "Someday I'm going to be running this place." You might never climb that high, but human nature says that you are going to at least try.

It is the same with authors who write stories and post them on sites like Literotica. Their first stories might not be all that good, but comments and feedback along with a desire to get better drive them toward putting out a better product or to at least try.

I'm no different. My first stories might not have been all that great, but they are still there on the hard drive. I like cheating wife stories and five years ago I found my first adult site that catered to cheating wife stories. It was a pay site, but it had a policy of giving a free lifetime membership to anyone who submitted five stories to the site. How hard can that be I said to myself as I sat down and fired up the word processor and went to work.

I sent my five stories in and sat back to enjoy my free membership and a funny thing happened. I started getting feedback, most of it positive, and I became hooked. I started cranking out more stories. The site I was sending my stories to had seven categories:

Bisexual
Cream Pie

Groups
I Watch
Gang Bang
Racial
SM/BD

I know nothing about bisexual or SM/BD and I had no interest in Groups so all the stories I wrote I tailored for the four remaining categories:

Cream Pie
I Watch
Gang Bang
Racial.

I turned out eight stories a month, two for each category, which means that after five years I have over 120 stories in each of those categories and they are all still on the hard drive.

A year ago I received an email asking me why I never posted stories on Literotica. The answer? I didn't know about Lit. I pulled it up, liked what I saw, and started sending in stories to it. All new stories? No, not hardly, not with over 400 stories sitting on the hard drive. Maybe one new story for each fifteen or so old ones. The newer ones are better, at least I think they are and I have received some feedback that leads me to believe that others think so too, and I will continue to write new ones.

But I am still going to recycle what is on the hard drive, stories that were written specifically to fit the four categories. That means that those of you who hate cream pie stories still have eighty or so to look forward to. Ditto for those who call me a racist; you will get another seventy or so interracial stories.

Those who hate wimps will only see about fifty more of those because the stories I sent to the I Watch category were split 50/50 between what some call wimps and some call "real men." Why the 50/50 split? It came from listening to the readers. I would get feedback asking me why all the men in my stories were hard asses. "In real life men are more forgiving, especially if it is the first indiscretion." So I would write stories with forgiving husbands and boyfriends and then the next batch of feedback would say, "Why are all your husbands spineless wimps" and I'd write stories that went back the other way.

Eventually I came to realize that I was wasting my time - there was no way I could write a story that would satisfy everybody and that is when I adopted my philosophy of writing for my own enjoyment and then offering to share.

As far as the gangbang stories? Well, what can I say? Gangbangs are gangbangs and there are still eighty or so of them to go.

The bottom line is that Literotica readers are going to see more of my old stories than my new ones. If I'm still around three or four years from now it will probably go the other way, more new than old.

I feel the need to respond to some of the comments and emails I have received. By far the largest percentage comes from people who say, "You are an asshole because all women are not whores and sluts and that's all you make them out to be."

Next most common is, "You must really hate women you sick fuck."

"You must be a wimp because all the men in your stories are wimps" is up there in the top ten along with, "Why don't you give it a rest and go crawl off in a hole somewhere."

There is a lot more, but I'm only going to address those four and in reverse order.

I won't stop and go crawl in a hole because I am enjoying the hell out of what I am doing and remember what I said, I am doing this for MY OWN ENJOYMENT and then I offer to share. Some obviously like my sharing with them and so I will continue to do so. No one is holding a gun to a reader's head and telling them they must click on a Just Plain Bob story or die. It is a conscious choice on the reader's part to move that mouse and click on that story.

When a man finds out he has a cheating wife or girlfriend there are only a limited number of ways he can handle it. If he loves her he can forgive, try to forget and try to hold on and somehow make things work. He can turn his back on her, walk away and get on with his life. The third option is to take revenge.

According to a good portion of those who send me feedback the first and second options are proof that the men are wimps. If the man takes the third option he is still considered a wimp if he doesn't do some sort of physical damage to the woman and her lover. These readers believe that the only way not to be a wimp is to kill, maim and destroy everything in sight. Doing that however, will invariably get the man throw in jail and that is why it so rarely happens in real life.

In real life most revenge takes place in the man's head when he says to himself, "I should have _____ (fill in the blank) the fucking cunt!" I know this because I have been there and done that (see The Dark Trilogy). In my stories I try to mirror real life so kill, maim and destroy are going to be for the most part absent. Outside of some fisticuffs there will be very little physical violence in my stories. Most of my husbands are going to do what I did, what several of my friends and others that I know have done, forgive, or walk away. If this makes them wimps and me a wimp for writing the story that way, so be it.

Next is the "I must hate all women." Nothing could be farther from the truth. I love women. I lust after women. I even like whores and sluts. I have been married four times, engaged two other times (that did not end in marriage) and I have always had girlfriends between marriages. My philosophy is that women were put on this earth for me to enjoy and I'm not talking just sexually. I could sit at the mall (and have) for hours and just girl watch.

The engagements, girlfriends and three of the four marriages bring me to the #1 anti JPB comment on the list.

"You are an asshole because all women aren't whores and sluts."

Well dear reader, you can not prove that by me! I will say up front that I KNOW all women aren't whores and sluts, BUT the majority of the women in my life were. My mother ran around on my father for years while he was driving a truck for a living. My Aunt Margaret cheated regularly on my Uncle Bill, as did my Aunt Mildred on my Uncle Paul. My Aunt Betty fucked around on my Uncle Bob for years and finally left him for his brother, my Uncle Wendell. Uncle Wendell in turn caught her on her knees at his company Christmas party giving Season's Greetings to his boss.

My sister is three times divorced and each divorce came about when the then current husband caught her out spreading pollen. Both of the engagements I mentioned ended when I found out that I was not the one and only and a lot of the girls I dated between marriages never made it to engagement status for the same reason.

And that brings me to my three ex-wives. The first one, Helen (I believe I commented on her in the intro to The Dark Trilogy) had seven different lovers before I found out what was going on. I was living proof that love is blind. Ditto with my second wife. She had a secret life that she hid from me and when I found out about her brother, his friends and the gangbangs she was history.

My third marriage ended in divorce because of a different kind of cheating (and I can just imagine the outrage I am going to get over this) - she cheated on me with an idea. I was away from home on business, she was lonely, a couple of Jehovah's Witnesses knocked on the door and my wife, with nothing better to do invited them in. When I came home from my trip I found out that she had found God. On a scale that runs from TRUE BELIEVER on one end to ATHEIST on the other you will find me just to the right of AGNOSTIC and since I would not allow myself to be SAVED the marriage eventually died.

So yes, I write about sluts and whores because as everyone knows, you tend to write about the things you know. And I do like sluts and whores, just not the ones that lie to me and cheat on me.

So be forewarned - if you click on a Just Plain Bob story you will be getting sluts, whores and husbands who do not kill, maim and destroy. There are other things you will rarely find in a Just Plain Bob story. Even though I try to mirror real life my stories all take place in StoryLand. In StoryLand STDs and unwanted pregnancies do not exist unless the author feels like they may add something to the story. Bad things do not happen in StoryLand unless the author so wills it and no amount of "You should have…" in comments and feedback will change a story already posted.

Lastly, I will touch on a truth. None of what I have written here means shit because the same readers will still read the same stories that they profess to hate and make the same comments they have always made. Knowing this, I will deliberately post stories that will have them frothing at the mouth.

It is the least I can do for an adoring public.

Thank you!

Just Plain Bob
justplainbob@awesomeauthors.org

You may also like the books by these authors:

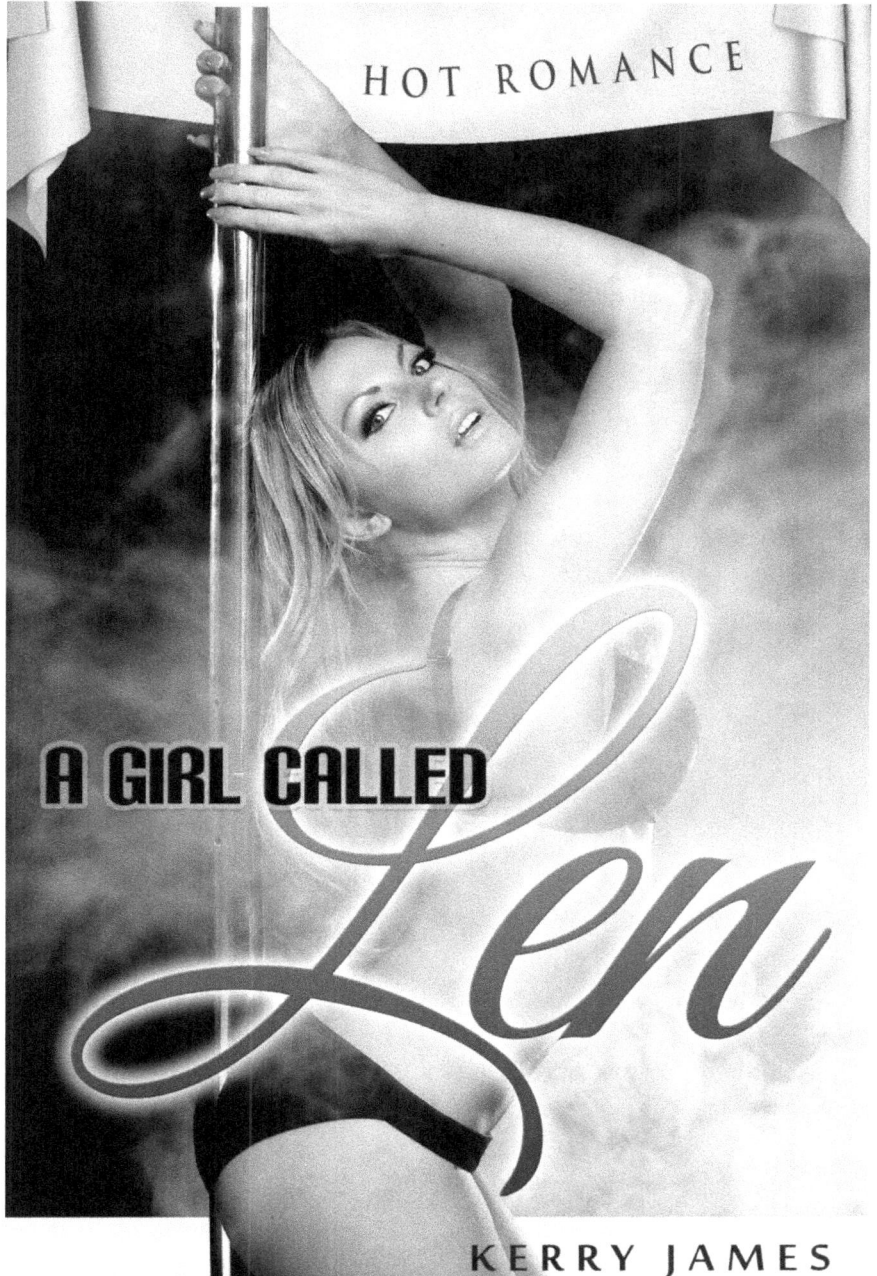

HOT ROMANCE

A GIRL CALLED

Len

KERRY JAMES

We had both lived and grown up in a little town just to the east of London. I suspect our first meeting was when there was a street party to celebrate the ending of the war with Germany. After that, all the kids in the avenue hung around together. It was strange really, suddenly there were all these friends, none of whom I had known about during the hostilities. I was six at that time and Len was five. I cannot remember why I called her Len, her name was really Leanne, but for whatever reason it stuck with me, and she seemed to be quite happy for me to call her that.

"Where was it you went to?" She was referring to the day my whole family uprooted and moved to the west. My dad had got a good job down there.

"Exeter," I replied.

"Are you still there?"

"Yes. Well I work in Exeter, but I live in a village about six miles away. What about you? Are you still at home, married, engaged, or something?"

"No, to the first. No, to the second, No, to the third. As for the something, I don't know. What about you? Are you married?"

"Yes." Did I see a wave of regret cross her face? I doubt it.

"So why are you up here in London?"

"My company has sent me on a course, to learn how to program this new machine they are bringing out."

She looked impressed "Oh, and what sort of machine is that?"

"It's an accounting machine. Businesses keep their bought and sales ledgers on them."

"I have seen those," she said this with a note of triumph in her voice. "I was temping and got a week's work in this office, doing filing, and they were using them. Noisy things aren't they?"

I had to agree, "They are, but this one won't be. It's all electronic, just whirrs. The noisiest thing about it is when it prints the ledger cards."

We were just making noises, fencing around before getting to the real issues. Len struck first. "So you decided to have an evening at a strip club?"

"Yes," I replied.

"Go often?" She was sounding like my mother who had interrogated me often on what I had been doing.

"First time," I admitted.

"Of all the joints in the world, you had to come into mine," she drawled like Humphrey Bogart. Then she asked the killer question.

"Why?"

"Because I wanted to see what a real live woman looked like in the nude."

She sat back in her chair with a look of shock on her face. "But Danny, you said you were married!"

I had to explain that which I was coming to believe, were the peculiar circumstances of my marriage. Len found it difficult to believe.

"You poor bugger!" I was shamefaced. Len went on, "It doesn't sound to me as if you have much of a marriage." Now perhaps I knew that already, but I wasn't going to allow others to comment on my marital circumstances.

"Oh, and as you are not married, you're the expert?" She saw the anger in my face and backed off. She reached across and again put her hand on mine. I liked her touch.

"Sorry, Danny. That was a stupid thing to say, especially from someone who does what I do. How could a stripper know what is normal or not in marriages? I've never had any kind of relationship."

I was intrigued at that. "What, never?"

Len shook her head. "Never. It sounds incredible, doesn't it? Here I am taking my clothes off, and showing everything to men, and I have never had any kind of relationship with anyone. No one's got into my knickers." Then she laughed, "Apart from you that is."

If you enjoyed this sample then look for **A Girl Called Len**.

JACK RYDER
HOT EROTICA

TAKE
THREE
MR. WRITER

It was 10:35pm when I let Victoria into my suite. Chloe was hiding in the bedroom closet with the hand held video camera all ready to record the evening events. April was hiding behind the kitchen counter that was out of view from anywhere in the suite unless you went directly into the kitchen area. She had the second burner cell phone that the video would be copied on from the camera that Chloe would be using. Jenny was underneath the bed in the bedroom with a very small but powerful audio microphone so we could record every word that would come out of Victoria's mouth.

"You are so gorgeous, Victoria," I announced as we came in the door. "I'm flattered that you want to do this with me." That was the cue to start the video and audio recording. "I bet that there have been many men that have wanted to have you," I stated coyly. Victoria was beside herself with pride as she told me that she has fucked three professors, two football coaches and the starting 12 offensive players of the football team.

"I can't believe that three professors would risk their positions for a one time chance with you." Without hesitation, Victoria blurted out their names. Then she even told me exactly WHEN the hook ups occurred and the name of the hotels that they used. "You must be really good in bed for those three old men to risk their jobs and marriage for." I chuckled inside as I stroked her pride. "But I still find it hard to believe that two coaches would have time away from their busy schedule to bang you," I teased her. She again named the coaches as well as where it happened and exactly when. "Wow, you really have been a busy girl," I smiled broadly. "But how on Earth did you manage to fuck the entire starting twelve football players?" I coaxed as I pushed her back onto the bed. "They paid me to have a party with them," she announced proudly as I pulled off her heels and began to remove my shirt. "You mean...they PAID you to fuck them?" I made my voice sound incredulous. Victoria had her eyes glued to the bulge in my shorts as I dropped my pants and kicked them off.

"Oh Yes, they did," she moaned as I pushed my shorts down to expose my throbbing prick. "They rented a fancy suite like this and took turns coming to the bedroom to fuck me," she nearly moaned it as she stared at my cock. "They each gave me $100 after they fucked me and they all said I was the best fuck they ever had," she told me triumphantly. "And it was fourteen if you count the punter and placekicker," she added with a giggle.

I now had all the damning information that I would need to end her threats. From this point forward I would use her as my plaything and punish her for her attempt to blackmail me. "Roll on your tummy, baby...I'd like to take a look at that gorgeous ass," I told her softly. Once she was on her stomach, I pulled the zipper down on the side of her skirt then ripped it all the way down till her skirt came apart and fell off. I yanked it out from under her and threw it on the floor.

"Do you enjoy reading my stories," I asked her softly while I gently fondled her gorgeous ass cheeks. "Oooh Yes Jake, I've been reading your stories since I was a little girl," she gasped as I slid my hand between her legs to finger her gash gently. "I used to steal them from my mother and...Play with my cunny while I read them in my room," she confided with a soft moan as I pressed a finger up into her dripping snatch. "Oooh Jake," she purred.

"Have you ever noticed that the main character in my dirty books loves to fuck his hookers up the ass?" I pressed my thumb straight up her ass when I said it. Her body was vibrating as I rammed my fingers and thumb in and out of both her holes. "Have you noticed that he loves to pull out and urinate all over those whores when he's done?" I growled in her ear as I bent forward. "Is that what you want? You want to be MY whore like you were for those boys? You want me to fuck you up the ass and piss all over you?" I bit on her earlobe after I finished whispering in her ear.

"No Jake...Please...I just want this...to be special. Just this once." Her entire body was writhing on the bed as I continued to shove my fingers in and out of her pussy and ass. SLAP...the force of my smack on her ass cheek left a glowing red imprint. "Okay, roll over and spread those legs for me then," I groused as I yanked my fingers out of her.

I ripped her blouse open as soon as she was flat on her back. "Did you enjoy fucking those fourteen boys," I growled as I slipped my dick up into her drenched slit. "Oooh Yes Jake. Yes," she groaned. "When you get paid to fuck that makes you a whore." I pulled my dick out then slammed it back in. "Are you MY whore Victoria?" Her body shuddered. "Oh Yes Jake, Yes I am," she groaned. I could feel the gush of her arousal as she shuddered again. As I humped my dick into her I sucked two hickeys onto her neck and then three more on her left tit.

Smack, Smack, Smack, Smack...as I slammed into her as hard as I could, I raised up with my arms to gaze at her pinned beneath me. Her tits jiggled and her body bounced on the bed as I pounded into her over and over. "Tell me you are MY whore," I grunted as I felt the orgasm building up in my nuts. "Tell my girls...you are my whore," I shouted. "YES JAKE, I'M A WHORE, I AM YOUR WHORE," she screamed as her body jerked into climax. I yanked my dick out of her and scooted forward so I could spray my load of cum all over her face and chest.

If you enjoyed this sample then look for **Take Three, Mr. Writer**.

DEXTER'S
Renaissance

LEE NORTH

Hot Romance Erotica

That May picnic was the beginning of a series of dates that Michelle and I enjoyed. Sometimes to a movie or play, often for dinner, occasionally for a ballgame. It was on one of those dates that there was a distinct shift in our relationship. Until then, we had held hands, kissed lightly, and generally behaved ourselves. I think we both could feel the pressure building. It changed after we had spent a pleasant evening at a local play.

We were in her late model Lincoln and I was driving. In the past, I would stop at the Rossmoor and she would drive on to her apartment. That night she had other ideas.

"Drive to my place, Dex. It's Friday, and we've got all weekend. You haven't been to my place yet and I'd like to spend some time with you," she said, placing her hand over mine.

It didn't take me any time at all to agree and head toward Lakeshore Drive. As we neared the building, Michelle took a small transmitter from her purse and pushed a button. The open grilled gate began to rise and I drove into the underground parking area as she directed me to her numbered space. The transmitter also unlocked the door to the elevator and stairs. After waiting a moment for an available car, a door slid open and we entered with Michelle inserting a card and pushing a button marked "R."

When we stepped out of the car, a large glass window was directly in front of us and I could see we were at the top of the building. To the left was 2102 and to the right, 2101. Michelle guided me right and opened the door, stepping in and turning on some lights.

It was a very nice and apparently large penthouse suite, one of two on the top floor of the building. As I looked around I saw the trappings of affluence; fine furniture, interesting artwork, and lush carpeting.

Michelle kicked off her shoes and I followed suit.

"Dex, I'm all sticky from the humidity today. I'm going to have a shower and change. Why don't you do the same, then we can relax and get to know each other better," she smiled.

I wasn't about to decline the offer and happily agreed. She led me to the main bathroom, handed me some towels and a washcloth and told me how to work the controls on the shower system. I needed the lesson. It was a multi-head system with pre-selected temperatures. The cabinet itself was almost as big as the bathroom in my apartment.

As I soaped and rinsed, I almost expected that Michelle would suddenly appear and join me, but that didn't happen. I stepped out of the shower, towelled myself off, and dressed in my slacks and shirt. I didn't bother with socks. They wouldn't be as fresh as I was so I stuffed them in my back pocket as I headed barefoot for the living area.

Waiting for Michelle, I wandered about the spacious penthouse. There was a dining area with a very nice buffet and china cabinet, along with a large period-style table and chairs. The kitchen was through a wide passage and it too was large, with a big island and plenty of cabinet and counter space. Most houses didn't have this much room.

I was just coming out of my inspection of the kitchen when Michelle reappeared and got my undivided attention. She was wearing a black silk pyjama suit, if that's what it's called. It was floor length, very sleek with material flowing from its wide legs and arms. She had a smile for me as she approached, then stopped and swirled in a circle to emphasize the graceful lines of her attire.

"You like?" she asked, already knowing my answer.

"Very nice … very elegant." I almost added very sexy. As she had moved to show off the garment it was immediately apparent that she was wearing nothing beneath it. Her nipples protruded clearly in front and her buttocks were perfectly outlined in back. I could feel my erection beginning to develop.

"Would you care for coffee … or perhaps a glass of wine or brandy?" she asked in a tempting tone.

"I'd like a glass of brandy, please."

"Oh, good. I'll have one too," she said, turning to move into the kitchen.

I followed her as if she was drawing me along. Perhaps it was the magnetic appeal of her, dressed as she was in such alluring garb. She reached up in a cupboard for the brandy bottle and I stepped behind her to help her. I was directly behind her now, touching her slightly with my hips and chest. On the spur of the moment, I did something I would never have thought I would do.

With the fingertips of my right hand, I lightly, slowly, ran them up her side, feeling her ribs as I went. Then, in a moment of complete recklessness, I moved my hand and gently cupped and stroked a fulsome breast. I felt her shiver from the contact but she didn't push me away or resist my touch. In fact, I was sure I heard a soft moan.

I couldn't see her face, but she had begun to lean back into me, the brandy bottle now forgotten. Her hands were on the countertop as if bracing her against an assault. My left hand joined the right in teasing her nipples and now her groan was more audible. Emboldened, I allowed my left hand to slip down over her abdomen and softly rub the silky smooth material of her gown.

I felt her backside push slowly back into me and she could certainly now feel my erection. I moved my hips to place my hardened member between her cheeks. She welcomed that with a swaying motion that only reinforced my hardness. One of us was going to have to do something soon.

It was Michelle who took my right hand and guided it inside her top, giving me access to her breasts. She pulled at the fold of the material and I felt a little pop as a small snap released the upper half of the garment. Still holding my hand, she slid it down to her waist where another small snap gave way and the gown parted completely.

I felt her shrug her shoulders and the lovely black item fell at her feet. She was naked before me, still facing away but leaning back more urgently against me, pressing herself into my prominent manhood. Once more, I did something I would not have thought I could attempt. I intimated with my knee that I wanted her to spread her legs and she immediately complied. She understood exactly what I was intending.

I unbuttoned my pants and they too fell at my feet, my briefs following them almost immediately. I took my cock in my hand and began to stroke her already wet centre in preparation for my entry. Again, she did everything she could to help me and within a few moments I was pushing into her. Slowly and carefully at first, but her insistence gave me courage to thrust a little more and soon I was buried well inside her.

I moved a little more forcefully and quickly as she continued to encourage me. There was absolutely no doubt in my mind that this was what she had planned all along. Her voice soon joined the action, not so much with words but with little cries of encouragement and pleasure. How long it had been since she had been with a man I did not know. I only knew she was with me now, and I was reaping the reward of her pent up need.

I leaned my head forward and captured an earlobe between my lips, then licked the back of her neck as I continued to stroke into her. In response, she threw her head back, growling a pagan, earthy moan of lust, slamming her ass back into me, the smacking sound of our joining now growing louder. This was probably going to end quite soon, but I did whatever I could to hold off as long as possible.

A few moments later her moves became more erratic and we almost fell out of rhythm as she began her orgasmic journey. I stayed with her as long as I could, but I was going to finish as well and there was nothing I could do to prevent it. I felt myself release into her once, twice, then a third time. As I did, she sagged against me and I wrapped my arms around her waist so that she didn't collapse against the granite counter or on the floor.

In all my experience, limited as it might have been, I had never had a more erotic, spontaneous coupling than this. I was in no condition to continue. Michelle was leaning back into me, breathing heavily and holding my arms tightly as they encircled her. Not a word had passed between us from the time she walked to the liquor cupboard.

I'm still not sure what got into me that night. I was either very confident of myself or very reckless. Probably the latter. Nonetheless, I picked the naked beauty up in my arms and carefully steered my way out of the kitchen toward the master bedroom. When I arrived, I saw that the bed had been turned down and I carefully laid Michelle on it crosswise with her legs dangling over the side. Her eyes were open and she was staring at me, no doubt wondering what I was doing. Still, neither of us had yet spoken.

I pulled off my shirt and now as naked as she, I got on my knees on the lushly carpeted floor, my hands gently but insistently pushing her legs apart. Again, she offered no resistance. I moved between her thighs and began to kiss the flawless, smooth skin. I was about to work my way up to the place where I had just planted my seed when I felt her hands in my hair. Was this a 'stop' or a 'go?'

I could see a bit of my semen on the lips of her vagina and I wondered what possessed me to try this. What was I trying to prove? Yet, even with that question in my head, I continued. As Michelle realized what I was planning, she must have had second thoughts. That had prompted her to place her hands on my head again, trying to decide if she should put a stop to my intentions. As I made up my mind to continue, I felt her resistance lessen.

I moved toward my target and slowly, with the flat of my tongue, I began to make love to her once again. This was going to be a very different kind of penetration. I had plenty of experience with oral sex but none just after I had planted my seed inside a woman. It was too late to stop now, and Michelle was making no sign that she wanted me to.

In fact, I was bringing her back to life with my tongue and fingers. Her hips were rising and falling erratically, responding to whatever stimuli she felt. Her grip on my head tightened and I could feel her fingers in my hair. She was holding on tight, her body dancing to whatever music my tongue created. I flicked the tip of her clitoris and got the response I expected. Her hips snapped up in reaction.

I was beginning to tire … or at least my tongue was. Michelle was nearing another orgasm and I willed myself to continue. At last she let go and I could stop and rest. I crawled up beside her, lying on my back. She rolled over me and gave me a deep, soulful kiss. Whatever I had accomplished, she approved of it. I wondered if it was something her late husband had not provided.

We lay there for a while, her head on my shoulder, our legs dangling over the edge of the bed. I kissed her forehead and ran my fingers through her soft, flowing hair. Her hand was holding my now flaccid cock, not manipulating it, just holding it lightly.

"That was wonderful," she said at last. "I didn't realize just how much I wanted you and you were perfect for me."

"We took some chances tonight," I said. "That gown didn't leave much to the imagination."

"It was either that or I would just come out naked. It was a coin toss."

"Were you worried I wouldn't get the message?"

"That thought did cross my mind. I can never be sure just what you are thinking about when it comes to women, Dex. Sometimes shy, but tonight a completely different person. You took command and I was the lucky one when you did."

"You were irresistible. I'm sure that was your plan, wasn't it? Well, it worked. I couldn't resist you, so everything that happened was a result of that."

"You'll stay tonight, won't you?"

"Yes. You might regret it in the morning, but I do want to stay. I want to wake up with you."

"We've started something, haven't we?" It was as much a statement as a question.

"I hope so. Is that what you want?" I wondered.

"Yes. As little as I know about you, as little time as I've known you, everything I've learned tells me that you are right for me."

"Well, we're going to have some time to find out so let's enjoy ourselves and see where it goes. I'm not a one-night-stand kind of guy. I'm looking for something more than that."

"You wouldn't be in this apartment tonight if I thought otherwise. But now that you're here, I'm going to keep you here as long as I can."

After a few minutes, Michelle rose and padded to the ensuite bathroom, closing the door behind her. She returned a minute or so later and crawled on top of me, rubbing my still limp cock with her lightly haired sex. I began to respond to her tantalizing little game and she noticed.

"Oh ... isn't that nice. Can I have some more please, sir?"

"Of course you may. Just tell me your heart's desire, young lady, and I'll try and fulfill your wishes."

"Well, after that glorious fucking you gave me in the kitchen, I think I'd like you to make love to me. Something nice and slow and lasting."

"How would you like me to start? A little foreplay, perhaps?"

"I think I've had all the foreplay I can handle tonight, Dex. I'm still carrying some of you around in me and what I really want is to have you inside me again."

If you enjoyed this sample then look for **<u>Dexter's Renaissance</u>**.

SAVING
Heather

HOT ROMANCE EROTICA
LILITH JONES

She went into his arms. Her kiss had been intended to be a light acceptance of his niceness. He kept it up, though, and she certainly had no reason to end it. He sucked her lower lip, and then he licked her lips. She opened them to him, but he kept licking them. She finally sought his tongue with hers. When they met, sparks flew. He pulled her to him, and she felt his firmness against her stomach.

"Oh, my love," he said when they broke. His hands went to the buttons on her blouse. She was his, and she let him strip her. He did it slowly, kissing every newly revealed inch of skin. She felt aroused, more aroused than she had been in years. She also felt cherished, cherished as not even the Rick of years ago had cherished her.

When he was kneeling and he had her jeans down around her ankles, he eased back to let her step out of them. Then he kissed her legs upward to her panties. He kissed her mound through those panties, and she felt ready for him. He eased her down on the bed.

If he'd been patience personified in removing her clothes, he was nearly a blur in removing his. Then he faced her, fully nude and magnificently male. He looked as ready for her as she felt ready for him. She pushed the panties down, and Rick took them off her feet. She spread her legs slightly as he got into bed.

He started with a kiss, though. It was a gentle, but extremely sensual, kiss. She arched her hips off the bed as their tongues met. He cupped her, holding all her femininity. As he moved his mouth from hers to her breasts, her nipple strained upward towards his mouth. He licked it, touching only the tip with the tip of his tongue. She quivered all over, and he moved to the other breast. When he sucked that nipple, sparks shot from the tips of her toes.

He thrust one finger deep inside her. Then he drew it out, very slowly, and over her clit. It was only one finger, but it went so slowly that it felt much more -- maybe a yard long. He changed breasts again and sucked deeply. The sucking and the stroking were sending heat through her. She felt as though she was being baked, and there was a fire in her womb.

He raised his head from her breast and stared into her eyes. "Heather," he said. "Heather, my love."

Then lightning crackled within her. She moaned and writhed. It went on as he kept stroking. She collapsed, and he removed his finger. He kissed her forehead and her shoulder. As her breath eased, he kissed her nose tip, and then her breasts, and then her stomach.

He again stroked her mound. He rubbed the lips there against one another, very softly. The response, however, was fire. His hand was wonderful, and his look was loving if it was searching. He had brought her delight, and she could believe he would bring her more delight. She wanted more than that, though.

"You," she said. "Please!" He rolled away suddenly. She stifled a protest when she saw that he was reaching in his drawer. She almost told him that he didn't need the rubber. She could tell, though, that this was one more act of caring. He was taking responsibility, taking care of her. Whatever the physical shortcomings, she would celebrate it as an action of the man who would never put her at risk.

Now, he was kneeling between her legs. She spread her lips with her hand and rolled her hips to receive him fully. She felt open to him.

"Heather," he said.

"Yes, oh yes."

However open she had been, she felt him stretch her more as he went in slowly. And it was slow, agonizingly slow. When he had filled her, he kissed her briefly. She hugged him with her arms and with her legs. He was in her, but she wanted to hold all of him.

He withdrew as slowly, and he felt a need for him to return. He thrust in a little faster, and she felt herself burn. As he sped up, it was never fast enough. She thrust up to engulf him as he came down. Then the lightning crashed through her again.

He withdrew half way, rammed into her, and pulsed deep within her. For a second, he was one rigid arch within her hug. Then he collapsed onto his elbows. She, too, relaxed. Her feet rested on his calves, and her hands rested on his back, but she was no longer really hugging him.

That was closeness. They were one. She was disappointed when he moved away, although the freedom to breathe was a relief. He moved off the bed and turned off the overhead light. As he came back, she heard the rubber drop into the wastebasket.

"We really need another pillow," he said as he got into bed. He lay down beside her and pulled her into a hug. He carefully spread the sheet over both of them.

"We don't really need a wider bed, though," she said. He chuckled. "Y'know . . . Maybe you don't know. I'm on the pill."

"Well, it didn't seem a good time to ask."

"It wasn't. You took care of me."

"I always will," he said. "Somebody should. You work too hard taking care of Anne. Somebody has to take care of you."

"Well, maybe, we'll take care of each other."

"That's a good idea. I love you. Seriously, if we're going to be a family, we'll have to divide up the family tasks. Probably, you should do the dividing. But give me some of the tasks of caring for Anne. Just because I don't know how, doesn't mean I can't learn."

"You do great. I might have to give her the baths and wash her clothes, but you give her kisses and protect her."

"Washing her clothes and yours can't be all that different from washing mine, and I wash mine already. Anyway, first you get the divorce, preferably with full custody. Next we get married. Then, if I can, I adopt her. After that, we'll try to get her to call me Daddy."

"I love you." Heather thought Rick's project to get Anne to call him Daddy reflected more of the story that she'd heard at the funeral than Anne's situation. Right now, Anne had two men in her life. One beat her, and she called him Daddy. The other hugged her, and she called him Rick. Anne would know which name meant love. Well, courts took forever, and four-year-olds were resilient. By the time Rick had gone through his agenda, Anne would call him anything he wanted.

"And I love you, too," Rick said. She believed him. His hand stroked up to her breast, and she patted it and held it there. "Is this what married people do?" he asked. "I mean lie in bed and talk later?"

"Well, I'm not sure that I want my last marriage to be a model." And that was an understatement. Too many of her conversations with Bill had been at the top of their lungs. "Is this what you want our marriage to be?"

"Yeah. Especially this part." He squeezed her breast very lightly. "I like holding you."

"And," she said in satisfaction, "I like being held by you."

If you enjoyed this sample then look for **Saving Heather**.

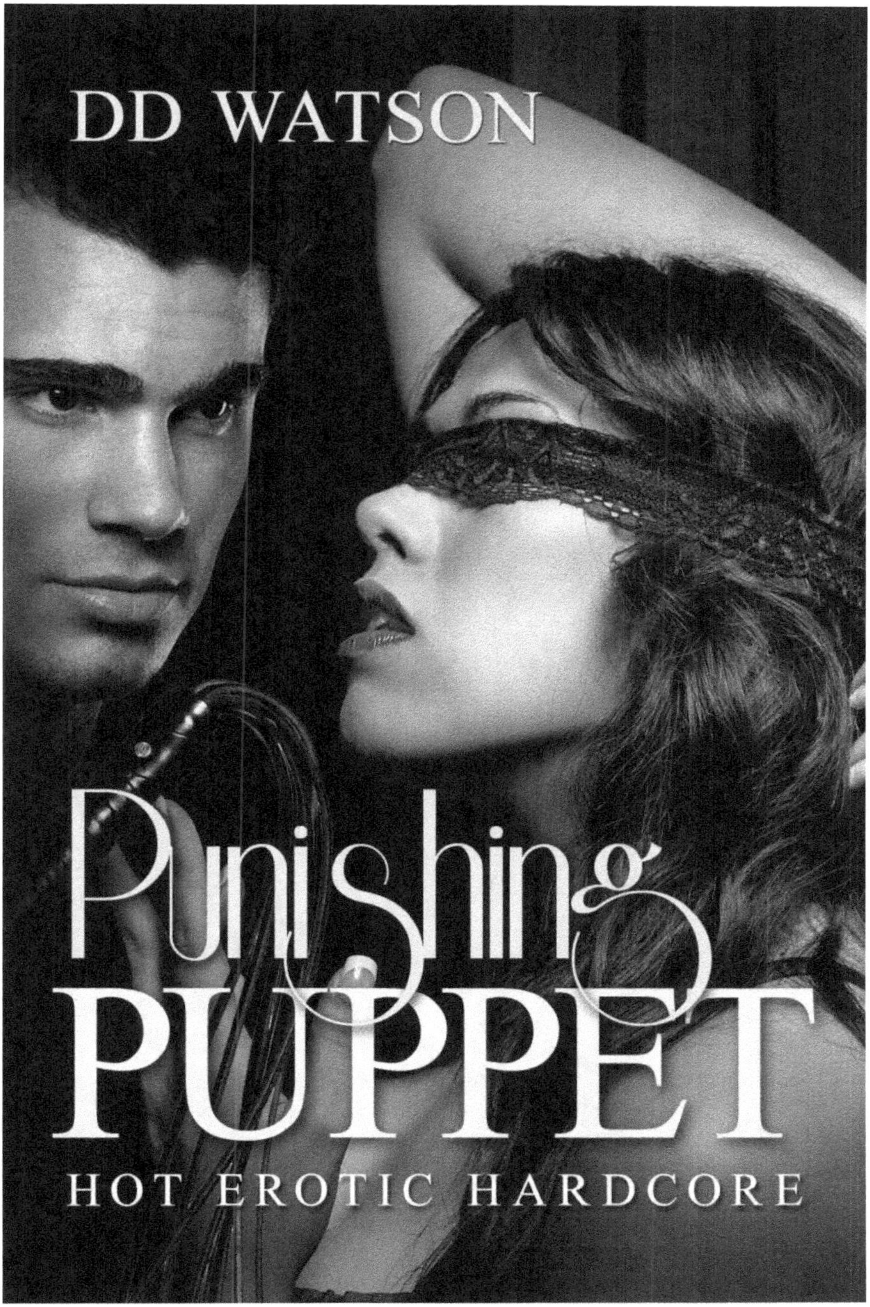
DD WATSON
Punishing
PUPPET
HOT EROTIC HARDCORE

Her head floated from side to side as she willed her eyes open. Her eyelashes parted to allow light in, but there was only darkness. The drug injected into her held her still even though her legs and arms were free.

She began to remember how she came to be where she was. The ride in the car trunk was by far bouncy but warm. When the trunk was open, her Master was there but didn't assist her out of it only his driver and another male she didn't recognize hauled her out. Before she could assess where she was the driver placed a patch on her neck, and her world went black again.

Puppet was never one to dwell on any negative situation. She trusted her Master Troy, no matter how mad he was with her breaking his rules he loved her unconditionally.

Going to the island was a set punishment but Puppet saw it as a learning experience. One she plans on succeeding in to make her Master proud.

She took in a deep breath and slowly exhaled it. That seem to help because she was able to move her fingers and toes sending a tingling sensation through her arms and legs. Puppet felt a growing chuckle inside her as if she was being tickled under her skin.

A smile spread on her cheeks as she tried to remain still to avoid another attack.

"You're awake," said the voice of a male that sat on the floor right beside her.

"Yes," she moaned. "You can see me?"

"Well yeah."

"So—it's not dark in here?"

"No it's very well lit you're just wearing a blindfold and the drug given to you is slowly wearing off."

"Oh, so where is the light coming from?"

"Window with a view of the garden showing a lovely sunny day."

"Why aren't you wearing a blindfold?"

"Because I'm here to watch you."

"Oh, so I'm on the island?"

"That is correct."

"Where's my Master Troy?"

"I'm not at liberty to say Puppet."

"And you know me. Am I allowed to be asking you questions?"

"With permission."

"By you?"

"No, by my Master—Shawn," he said, glancing up at the green eyed male who handpicked him out of a dozen. Took ownership, making him his personal pet; he stood clean shaven wearing black jeans, biker boots and shirtless. His long black mane hung loose on his shoulders. Two men stood behind him both wearing leather pants black boots and chest harnesses with buzz cut hairstyles.

"Is Master Shawn training me because I disappointed my Master?"

"He is."

"Is he listening to us?"

"Yes."

"Is he here in the room with us?"

He was signaled to silence by Shawn hovering his fingers in front of his pet's mouth. Shawn sat beside Puppet and leaned into her ear.

"I'm right here Puppet." His accent vibrated through her ears as she took in the heavenly scent that radiated from his skin.

Puppet enjoyed the tender time she was allowed to spend with him even though she hasn't laid eyes on him yet.

"That will be all Peter you may return to your duties."

"Thank you Master." On hand and knee Peter crawled out of the room followed by one of the males. Turning his attention back to Puppet, Shawn took his fingers and traveled over her naked skin, igniting the sensation that tortured her a moment ago.

Puppet tried to keep a straight face but regaining some movement in his limbs she began to squirm and giggle. Shawn only watched as she didn't try to push him away but seem to enjoy the torment. He watched her nipples harden as he flicked them with two fingers. Then running them between her legs he felt the wetness building in the soft folds of her crouch. He brought his drenched fingers to her mouth and pressed them pass her lips where she sucked and licked them clean. He removed them and rose to his feet.

"Get her to her knees on the floor and face her to the bed," he ordered a male who moved quickly to perform his task. Jerking Puppet up, he forced her into position as Shawn instructed.

Shawn walked over to a duffle bag opened in the corner and removed a handheld whip. The handle was as long as his arm with nine tails all knotted. When he returned his attention to Puppet, still blindfolded on her knees, he didn't hesitate. When the first strike landed she let out a deep cry that ricocheted around them. He landed another that resulted in the same. He picked up the tempo and continued to strike her back and arse until the welts glowed a profound red.

"How many blows did I give you Puppet?" He asked watching her claw at the mattress. "Answer me," he snapped striking her again.

"Six—teen—Master."

"Splendid, most pets never count. Troy has been training you."

"Yes Master—my Master is good to his pet."

"A little too good, or you wouldn't be here Puppet."

"Yes Master."

He switched the whip in his opposite hand and walked over to Puppet, snatching the blindfold from her eyes.

"Turn around Puppet and place your arms on the bed for support but remain on your knees."

"Yes Master." She turned clumsily but managed, getting her first glimpse of the notorious Shawn. The man whom her Master said strikes fear in any pet who crosses his path. Why was she not afraid? Was he just playing with her? She caught his emerald eyes, which shot ice daggers at her. His chiseled looks could rival her Master Troy's.

"Troy mentioned you were hard-headed. Who said you could look at my eyes?"

Puppet caught on, but it was too late as he began to whip her chest, stomach and thighs. The pain was more intense, but she kept her arm on the bed and didn't try to run away. Her Master Troy whipped her in this same manner on different occasions, so she grew to accept her punishments no matter how unforgiving they were.

When he stopped, she collapsed onto the floor at his feet breathing intensely but not unconscious.

"Take her to the groomers and tell them I'll call when I'm ready for her."

The male lifted Puppet up as if she didn't weigh a thing and draped her on his shoulder carrying her out of the room.

Peter had lied to Puppet, who was hanging upside down. She glanced around the room and saw no window only a ceiling light, mirrors and two doors.

Once Puppet was gone the second door opened, and Troy walked in wearing his full business attire. Shawn turned and smiled at his old friend from school whose dreams mimicked his.

"So what's your conclusion?" asked Troy.

"She's knows what she wants. I never saw a first timer take what she took from me. Or—maybe I've become soft."

"No, it's not you, Puppet is without doubt atypical. I can do anything to her, anything I wish."

"Then why bring her to me? Apparently you have a handle on her."

"No, she's become hesitant and explorative, not asking permission."

"She's evolving?"

"It has been five years. And as I said she'd taken my treatments without complaint."

"Do you want me to train her to be a dominatrix?"

Troy fell silent as he glanced to the floor. He closed his eyes and remembered his devoted pet and how she found him. Shawn's strong hand rested on his friend's shoulder waking him from his thoughts.

"It's been a long trip for you both, come and relax with me and let the groomer spoil her. A good meal, drink and sucking will clear your mind to make a decision."

That brought a grin to Troy's face as he let Shawn lead him out of the room.

If you enjoyed this sample then look for **Punishing Puppet**.

WANT FREE COPIES OF MY BOOKS?
Just visit my blog and download free copies of my books:

awesomeauthors.org/justplainbob

www.ingramcontent.com/pod-product-compliance
Lightning Source LLC
Chambersburg PA
CBHW051510170626
46811CB00002B/747